REFLECTIONS IN THE STREAM

REFLECTIONS IN THE STREAM

Spiros G. Frangos

ISBN 978-0-578-07933-2

For the loves of my life:

my wife Rosalia and my daughters Ioanna Leonora and Arianna Ekaterene

who every day help me maintain perspective by reminding me what those

very few things in life are that (actually do) matter

In loving memory of…
my father George

"if a man would guide his life by true philosophy, he will find ample riches in a modest livelihood enjoyed with a tranquil mind."

- Lucretius

Author's Note

No literary agent, editor, or publisher has altered this book in any way. If text or story arc appear unorthodox (or just not what you're used to), you're probably right.

To those who read deeply into every word and phrase searching for symbols, significance, or hidden meanings behind seemingly trivial text (and who ultimately convince yourselves that you have picked up on a subtlety that the next reader *must* have missed), you're probably right as well.

Finally, I value any thoughts, opinions, or criticisms, and I hope that when you finish the book, you might take the time to share some with me. (spiros.frangos@gmail.com)

****

Part I

New York City, 1998

Chapter 1

Thirty-six hours after my exposure, I arrived at Brigham's employee health services to get the results of my blood tests. Much like a patient with asthma, I couldn't take a full deep breath in as I walked up to the front desk to register. My hand was shaking. My signature seemed foreign.

I had never in my life been tested for H.I.V. or any hepatitis virus for that matter. As a surgical trainee, I was constantly dealing with blood and needles, and certain, albeit minor, exposures were the norm in the operating room. And then there was the reason I was there in the first place- the issue of the patient's blood: was it infected?

The nurse showed me to a small, dimly lit examination room where I sat on the patient's side of the matter holding my own hand. The cut on my right palm was clean with a rim of dried blood.

"Dr. Karos? Timos Karos?" The employee health internist walked in without knocking. A fuzzy goatee surrounded a forced smile. "Timos is your first name?"

"I go by Ty," I said.

"How are you doing today?" he said adjusting his white coat.

"OK," I muttered.

"So I have your lab tests here." He opened my medical folder and scanned the forms to be sure: "First of all, your H.I.V. test was negative." I let out the breath I had involuntarily held. "Your hepatitis B confirms you've been adequately immunized, and your hepatitis C is also negative, so *you* are starting off with a clean slate."

My chest loosened just a bit. I sat back on my chair.

"Now, I don't have the results of his hepatitis panel yet, but your patient's rapid H.I.V. test *is* back, and it's negative," he said emphasizing the final three words.

I smiled for a moment, but my core would have nothing of it. I felt my lips tapering and inverting. The room fogged up. "I'm sorry," I said, although I knew I had little say- the new me was unlike the old me.

"So now you've already started taking the anti-retrovirals?" the internist asked.

My face was burning. "Yes." I loosened my tie, unbuttoned the one at the top, and wiped the tears away with my fingers.

"Well, go ahead and stop them," he said. "Now again, I don't have the victim's hepatitis panel back yet, so we don't know if you've been exposed to the hep C virus. I need to see you again tomorrow."

Tomorrow? Another twenty-four hours of this? I was back in my own bed, wide-awake, staring up at shadows, thinking, analyzing, feeling sorry.

He saw it.

"Alright. Alright. Hold on. Let me call the lab and see what they have."

The door shut. The news so far had been all-good, but my subconscious couldn't keep up, couldn't adjust accordingly. I stood and looked into the mirror over the sink at the frightened little boy with the peaceful face and the curly head. Deep down, I understood that these intense feelings of fear were well-beyond rational, but I also knew there was nothing at all I could do about it.

****

Thirty-six hours earlier

The shuffling of my heavy wooden clogs along the hard linoleum floor sounded like the ticking of a large clock. I was practically shivering- the hospital's air-conditioning always seemed to be on full throttle on summer nights- as I wandered arms-crossed through the dingy halls of the surgical intensive care unit. It was after midnight, and at least one patient needed checking in on. My text pager broke the silence: "TRAUMA CODE." I sighed knowing my call room bed would remain untouched.

The elevator down to the emergency department was empty. I entered the trauma room, removed the white lab coat I wore over my blue scrubs and hung it on the side of the door.

"What've we got?"

The trauma nurse who had received the paramedics' notification was still fiddling with her walkie-talkie. "Multiple gunshot wound. Blood pressure: 50 over palp. Five minutes out." She never looked up.

"We got a chest tube ready? We got a thoracotomy tray? Don't open them but have them ready to go," I said.

I put on a yellow cloth gown, a pair of gloves, and a surgical mask with a clear visor to protect my eyes. My chief resident Ted Gorcki was operating on a perforated ulcer. Until he arrived, this was going to be my show. Staff started funneling into the room. There were nurses, medical students, emergency department physicians, hospital business associates, physician assistants, patient care personnel.

"Whoever doesn't need to be here, please leave," I said in a loud voice. "Whoever needs to be here, but isn't gonna be helping directly, please stand back against the wall."

The crowd obeyed, and the room became eerily quiet for the next few minutes. I stared down at the empty stretcher and recalled a time when *I* was on the other end of all this. Frozen except for racing thoughts, I stood there listening to my heart beat.

Two male paramedics on either side of a transport stretcher turned the corner and burst into the room. My attention shifted to a motionless, young Caucasian man with blood across his face, bare chest and abdomen. One of the two paramedics was a behemoth of a man- had to be over 300 pounds- drenched in sweat. His partner was administering chest compressions.

"He lost his pulse about three minutes ago," said the heavy paramedic breathing hard and fast. "OK folks, from the beginnin', we got a 22 year old kid, at least three bullet holes, one in his left chest, two in his abdomen. We got two fourteens, one in each antecube. We got no pulse. I repeat: three minutes of CPR so far."

"Bring him over," I said. Fourteen arms reached in and together we moved the flaccid body from the transport stretcher to the resuscitation stretcher. His skin was warm. His passing had not yet been agreed upon. "Anesthesia: let's get him intubated. Someone hand me the thoracotomy tray. Now!"

Controlled chaos erupted, as everybody tried to fulfill responsibilities. The anesthesiologists set up to place the breathing tube. The trauma nurse assessed for vital signs, while a second nurse and an intern stripped off what was left of the patient's clothing with heavy scissors.

"I have no groin pulse," the trauma nurse called out.

"Ted Gorcki's scrubbed upstairs," I said. "Can someone call there and make sure he knows what's going on?" Ted would be angry if he felt no effort had been made to reach him. Emergency department thoracotomies were uncommon, and the surgical chief resident needed to be made aware.

The algorithm was clear. I squirted some povidone-iodine solution onto the patient's left chest, lifted a scalpel off the instrument tray, and started a thoracotomy incision that extended from under his left nipple along the contour of the rib cage towards the left armpit. After a second and third pass with the knife, I opened a space between his ribs. Bright red blood gushed out onto the mattress, as I got my first look at his lung.

"Rib-spreader," I shouted for no reason other than the adrenaline pumping through my own circulation. This was my opportunity to bring a dead man back to life- my ongoing, selfish pursuit of instant, immediate gratification. Could I *catch* him? *Could I save him from annihilation?*

"Let me help." Already gowned and gloved, Ted stood across from me.

"Hold the lungs back," I said. "I'm just about to cross-clamp." With Ted's help, I placed a long clamp across the aorta in an attempt to divert blood to the patient's heart and brain.

"Open his pericardium! I think he's got tamponade," Ted shouted. "Give him the knife."

Ted was right. The chamber which houses the heart was swollen with blood, compressing the organ, not allowing it to fill and pump. I reached back towards the tray into which I had laid the scalpel and felt a sharp pain in the palm of my right hand.

"Careful. I'm sorry. I'm so sorry," a woman's voice quivered. I looked up at Eva, a medical student, standing near the patient's legs. Eager to help, she had heard Ted's order and raised the scalpel off the tray to hand back to me. Instead, she hovered it knife blade forward in the direct path of my outstretched hand. The blade dug into the middle of my palm, and blood was collecting under my glove.

Ted maintained his composure. "Give me another knife. Go wash your hands."

I stripped my gloves off and found a two-centimeter laceration seeping red. As I started towards the sink, I looked down at the scalpel, which was back on the instrument tray. A chill ran up my spine. The knife was saturated with blood- blood which wasn't all mine.

I washed my hands with soap and water. My forehead began to throb, the reality of a trigger sufficient to awaken my demons setting in.

"I'm calling it: one thirty-five AM," Ted said. He had performed advanced cardiac life support measures with manual compression of the heart for twenty-five minutes without success. I wasn't able to get back in to help since my cut continued to ooze, so I stood by the sink pressing on it firmly with a gauze pad.

"We tried," Ted said pulling off his mask and cap uncovering his big nose and bald head. "I knew it was bad as soon as I saw the paramedics walking out of the trauma bay. There're always two of 'em, and there's always a fat guy and a skinny guy. If the fat guy's sweating a lot, chances are the patient's sick. I don't even have to look down at the stretcher. I just have to look at the fat paramedic. The more he's sweating, the lower the blood pressure."

The ER attending was standing behind Ted waiting his turn. "I recognize this guy," he said with a stern look on his face. "He's been in and out of here a few times over the last couple of months. He's into needles- heroin."

"You have to be kidding," I said.

He shook his head. "I checked the computer to see if he's had an H.I.V. or a hepatitis panel here recently, but I couldn't find one."

"Don't worry," Ted said. "I've gotten stuck a dozen times over the last five years. The chances are really low."

"This guy's high risk," I said.

"I agree. I suggest you take the H.I.V. cocktail," said the ER attending. "Let's draw your blood first. We already sent off his with the rest of the labs, and I just added a hepatitis screen and an H.I.V. test. Apparently his mother and his girlfriend are in the waiting room. I'll go talk to them and get consent."

A nurse drew my blood for testing, while Ted gathered supplies to sew up my cut. He injected local anesthetic before re-approximating my laceration with five stitches. Through it all, I didn't say a word.

"We have a small quantity of these drugs down here for urgent use," the ER attending said. "You have to take them within an hour of exposure if you want any true prophylaxis. These are zidovudine, these are lamivudine, and these are indinavir. Take one of each now."

"Side effects?"

"Nausea maybe some diarrhea are the usual ones."

"I should have some results by tomorrow?" I asked.

"You should."

I taped a sterile gauze dressing onto my palm and walked to the lounge, where I poured a cup of water and swallowed each pill with a small sip. The last one was the size of a small battery, and I gagged trying to gulp it down whole. I dropped the bottles into my back pocket. It was almost four in the morning. Standing there alone, exhausted, and away from the commotion, I felt the sadness. For the first time in a decade, a familiar turmoil was brewing. I understood that all this was situational- a natural response to an unfortunate mishap- but I also knew rationalizing wouldn't help. Seasons were set to change, and I sensed *an unfavorable fall* approaching in haste. The horrible disturbance I held at bay every single day of my life was rearing its head, although, at least on this night, I refused to succumb to it. I took a deep breath and plunged back into the organized chaos of a big city hospital's emergency department.

****

A full half-hour passed. The internist barged in inadvertently slamming the door behind him. He didn't hesitate, not even for a second: "So he was hep C positive."

"No."

"Let me tell you exactly what this means," he said. "First of all, the hep C transmission rate from a needle-stick exposure is maybe three or four percent, so odds are you won't get it."

"Mine was a scalpel."

"I know," the internist said. "Now I can't give you an exact number since this is a less common injury, but if I had to guess from the way you described it, I'd have to say the risk is higher, maybe by five or ten fold, maybe in the..."

I was alone again. Despite many years of good work, no one had my back. God was nowhere. This didn't surprise me. I bit my lower lip and caught myself involuntarily shaking my head.

"Now what does that mean for you?" the internist said as I zoned back in. "There's no prophylactic treatment available to lessen your likelihood of getting the virus- seroconverting- like there is for H.I.V. I need for you to get tested at six weeks, three months, and then again at six months. If all these tests are negative, you're essentially cleared."

I felt my jaw quivering. *Fearing death wastes precious time. Again! Fearing death wastes precious time.* I've been through this before. *Fearing death wastes irretrievable time which can never be recovered.* I knew this- it was one of my own rules! But this was the one that gave me the greatest difficulty. The primitive notion that death is a terrifying *end* was impossible for me to reconcile.

"Most people who do convert," he said, "manifest within the first six weeks, maybe some abdominal pain, maybe some nausea and vomiting, and in some circumstances with acute hepatic insufficiency from the infection you may become jaundiced. Some people convert and have no symptoms at all, but they stay carriers and can still pass it on to others. Even if you do convert, transmission to someone else is unlikely, unless your blood contacts their blood like by shared needles."

"I thought hep C and H.I.V. are both transmitted in the same way- through blood," I said, "but they're also both found in secretions, so if you can get H.I.V. through sex, you should also be able to get hep C as well?"

"You're right. There has been reported sexual transmission of hep C, but there are no clear-cut recommendations in this area. For the most part, the CDC states that if you're monogamous, you can continue having relations with your partner even if one of you has hep C."

"That doesn't make sense. There's always that small possibility of transmission to a partner," I said.

He hesitated, then reluctantly: "Yes."

"So should we be advocating playing Russian roulette with someone else's life?"

"Now remember…"

"No, seriously, can I be with someone and have a clear conscience that I'm not gonna make her sick?"

"Are you married?" he asked.

"No."

"I can't say that the risk is zero if that's what you wanna hear," he said. "If you do get hep C, and you have a cut in your mouth or there are high levels of the virus in your saliva, yes, transmission's possible and the risk's not zero. You can pass it on to someone through kissing and sex, but it would be considered an uncommon event."

"Can I still operate? I'm not gonna lose a year?"

"You can still operate and take care of patients just like you've been doing as long as you continue to practice universal precautions and make sure you double-glove in the O.R." He stood and removed his white coat. "Hot in here?"

"And if I convert?"

"Same thing. You can continue to operate. We'll preserve all confidentiality," he sat back down. "We'll have to inform the hospital of your status, but unless you're found displaying gross negligence or sloppy technique, the administration won't take your privileges away, so..."

The internist's tie was not by chance- the image of a white lighthouse on a sandy beach surrounded by palm trees. Blue, frothy waves were spilling onto the shore battering the lonely beacon. God is indifferent about me. I have always known this to be true. I have accepted it and this has made me stronger.

"We're getting way, way ahead of ourselves," he said. "Chances are you won't convert, but you do understand we have to go through the motions. If you have no more questions, I'll see you again six weeks from now."

Chapter 2

It was a humid August morning as we made our way through the post-op care units at Brigham Hospital. My exposure wouldn't be for another two weeks. I was a different person. I was just beginning to peak. I couldn't have been happier.

Our team consisted of four surgical residents- of whom I was one- and three medical students. The final stop on morning rounds was the cardiothoracic intensive care unit. Our newest patient was twelve years old.

Tum...Fshhhhhhhhhhhhhhh

"Michael had practically his entire aorta replaced last night," Ted Gorcki whispered. "He dissected and was in the O.R. for nine hours."

Tum...Fshhhhhhhhhhhhhhh

In a full-size specialty bed with abundant room to spare lay a little boy. He had a breathing tube down his throat but was awake scanning our group with his eyes. He appeared comfortable. The ventilator cycled and filled his lungs: *Tum...Fshhhhhhhhhhh*, as his chest rose and fell in accordance. A young couple- maybe early thirties- sat by him with strained smiles. *Innocent victims. Why were they being challenged so young?* I rested my hand on the father's shoulder.

"How're you doing, Michael?" Ted asked.

Gagging with the tube in his airway, the boy delicately lifted one arm off the bed and extended two fingers. Ted smiled at the sight of victory.

"No pain?" I asked. Michael shook his head. "You're sure? No pain at all?" He shook his head again. "What he's getting right now seems to be working," I said to the father, "but let us know if he starts complaining and we'll up the dose."

Over in the corner of the room, sleeping in an awkward fetal position on a hospital armchair, was the cardiothoracic fellow who had participated in the surgery at the expense of a night's sleep. In the event of an acute deterioration, he would be readily available.

We funneled out of the room as the boy with a second chance gradually lowered his arm.

"*This* is why you guys should think about surgery," I said to the students as the team began to disperse. Eva- a nerd with no sense of hierarchy- seemed eager to hear the reason. "Surgeons *care* for their patients in both senses of the word."

"The cardiac fellow was up all night," she said. "Probably went twenty-four straight hours without sleep. That's torture, don't you think?"

"Torture?" I repeated. "There's nothing more satisfying. I mean what a difference he made in this little kid's life."

"But it's so hard to do anything else if you're in the hospital all the time."

"What's more important?" I said.

Eva followed me to the O.R.

"Ty, you're how old?" she said.

"Twenty-eight."

"And you're only in the middle of your training. It takes so long- so many late nights studying by yourself, endless hours on the wards, in the operating room. I don't think I could do that. You really gotta want it."

"No question. It's a huge investment. But taking care of surgical patients is much more rewarding than even I thought it would be when I was a med student."

"And how'd you know it was the right fit?"

"My personality. If you're an internist, you treat a patient with high blood pressure or emphysema over a lifetime- maybe you help them get better short-term, but in the end- most of the time- the disease wins. Surgery: you take the patient to the operating room, remove a mass, fix a defect. Instant results!"

"If you take out a ruptured appendix, a patient can't get appendicitis again."

"Exactly," I said. "On-the-spot satisfaction. A quick high."

"But the hours? Your lifestyle really takes a hit," Eva said.

She'll never get it. She'll never get me. The difficult lifestyle, the brutal training made me productive while restraining me from wandering into that compromised region of my brain. This was a critical perk. Keeping busy kept me sane.

"How'd you know you wanted to do medicine?" Eva said.

"Learning the anatomy, all the things that might go wrong with it, made me more comfortable."

"More comfortable with what?"

"The everyday. Trust me- focus on science above anything else. It'll make you a better person," I said.

We turned the corner and hung our white coats outside the O.R. suite.

"Did you have a mentor?" Eva asked.

"My great-uncle- he was also a doctor. He died a few years back."

"He helped you?"

The motion-sensing double doors swung open, and we walked through.

"Really set me in the right direction."

Uncle Timos had led me to the rules. Ten bullets. My secret weapon. Although the notion of not having added to the list in so long was upsetting, I knew all I needed was a little direction to secure the remaining four. From where or from whom this would come, I hadn't a clue.

****

Pre-dawn the following morning, I sat with Ted at the nursing station in the emergency department. Ted was two years ahead of me in his final year of the General Surgery residency program, but he never seemed to get much respect. He was a bland personality who was known to be technically challenged- not a good thing for a hands-on profession.

Ted's claim to fame among the residents was the 'cheesecake story.' While on an international flight, an urgent call for a doctor was placed to which Ted responded and found an elderly man slumped over in his seat unconscious. Ted suspected that the man might be unarousable on account of a medical condition, erroneously suspecting a low blood sugar. Ted didn't want to pour juice into the man's mouth fearing that he might choke and aspirate. Using his medical know-how and recognizing fully well that the rectum has a superb absorptive capacity, Ted eyed a piece of cheesecake on the adjacent passenger's tray table and thought that if he could shove some cake up the man's anus, he could correct the dangerously depleted sugar level and salvage the situation. Ted kneeled along the aisle and pulled the man's trousers and boxers down around his ankles, when the man who just happened to be a heavy sleeper woke up to find Ted's smiling face between his knees.

On this overnight call, Ted wasn't in the best of moods. The last twelve hours had been painful for both of us with one disaster after another. A homeless man in septic shock who was crashing in the I.C.U. A stoic Chinese man with six days of abdominal pain and a ruptured appendix who had decided to visit his acupuncturist first. A lawyer who had been stabbed eight times in the abdomen by his own son after an argument over the remote control. A nurse whose boyfriend perforated her rectum with his fist during a bout of violent, drunken sex. A teenager who accidentally shot himself in the groin with his own gun. And now Ted was most annoyed at the notion of having to call our attending Dr. Hobbes at home at four o'clock in the morning with bad news.

"Dr. Hobbes? Is this Dr. Hobbes? Sorry to wake you, sir. It's Ted. Ted Gorcki… Your chief resident, Ted Gorcki. Yes, your chief... Yes. Ted… It's about your patient Mr. Fann, the drug-abuser, post-op day three from a cholecystectomy. Well, he's not in his bed. No one can find him, sir. He seems to be missing. I'm not sure where he went, but we're actively looking for him." I watched as Ted's eyes widened. He lip synched 'What!' in my direction. "Yes, sir. Thank you. Sorry to wake you."

"What'd he say?" I asked.

Ted smiled. "Can you believe this guy?!"

"What'd he say?"

Ted shook his head and stroked his scalp with his fingers. "With his pompous little, freakin' English accent, he said, 'Well Dr. Gorcki, I can tell you one thing for sure, he's not here.'"

From what I had heard about the Oxford-trained Geoffrey Hobbes, he was a spectacular personality. Well-traveled with a taste for the finer things including art, literature, philosophy, cooking, and wine, he was successfully multi-dimensional unlike many physicians whose knowledge and interests are limited to their practice. Dr. Hobbes was an intimidating figure. He had authored over one hundred journal articles and two dozen book chapters. Clever with a proficient sarcasm, he welcomed the 'swordplay of the mind' and dueled to the death. 'In the battle of wits, I do not fight the unarmed,' he often told Ted. Rarely interacting with the juniors, I obliged by flying low under his radar. If I passed him in the hallway, he rarely acknowledged me or the insecure, under-my-breath 'hello' he invariably evoked.

"I hate that bastard," Ted said. Over the last two plus years, I had come to realize that Ted's opinion of Dr. Hobbes was a result of his own ineptitude. He was always on the losing end of the swordfight, and instead of learning a lesson or two from those interactions, his bitterness had merely grown.

Ted took off for the call room, while I had a few more things to take care of before morning rounds. My intentions were good, my fatigue greater.

****

"Will you be helping me, Dr. Karos?"

A man's voice. Funny accent. I raised my head off the desk. Dr. Hobbes was standing over me. A tall, slender gentleman- mid-sixties- with thinning, graying hair brushed straight back. His suit was buckingham blue enhanced by an open-collared crimson shirt with extra long sleeves exposing golden cuff links. I was surprised he knew my name but too disoriented to appreciate it.

"Good morning," I mumbled. The clock on the wall behind him read 6 A.M.

"Dr. Karos, surgery is like sex. It's interesting to read about. It's fun to watch. But nothing beats doing it." I had heard the aphorism before from another surgeon but with humor attached; coming from Dr. Hobbes' stoic demeanor, it sounded more like some dire life's lesson. "We have a case."

"You want *me* to scrub?" I asked. "On the Whipple?" Not only did most senior attendings operate preferentially with chief residents, but I also knew Dr. Hobbes had a pancreaticoduodenectomy on the schedule that morning. This operation- also known as a Whipple's procedure after the surgery's late pioneer- was performed for pancreatic cancer and involved the removal of portions of the small intestine and pancreas. It is one of the most technically challenging in all of general surgery.

Dr. Hobbes raised his eyebrows. His eyes widened. "'Operative skill cannot be gained by observation', young Dr. Karos, 'any more than skill in playing the violin can be had by hearing and seeing a virtuoso performing on that instrument'- this coincidentally was uttered by Dr. Whipple himself."

****

With the abdomen of our now common patient spread open between us, I wouldn't have noticed a parade marching behind me.

The skin had been incised with a scalpel along the midline curving around the bellybutton. The remaining tissues had been cut using an electrocautery pen, and the abdominal cavity had been entered and inspected. There was no evidence for obvious metastatic disease. The liver had been palpated and appeared fatty but otherwise normal. The stomach had been mobilized and retracted out of the way, while the bile duct and named blood vessels had been dissected free of surrounding tissues and controlled. Small bleeders had been cauterized. Large bleeders had been tied.

A full hour had passed. Except for some criticism- 'don't pass point with your instrument,' 'move along,' 'you're left hand is doing nothing'- there had been no conversation beyond the essential guidance. With Dr. Hobbes' gaze fixed on my every move, my hands were not in synchrony with my brain's demands. As the surgery turned more complex, my inexperience must have become apparent as Dr. Hobbes took over entirely.

Given my review of the surgical atlas in the twelve minutes I could spare between morning rounds and scrubbing, the surgery was proceeding routinely, although I couldn't help but wonder why he had wanted me there in the first place. Dr. Hobbes eventually decided it was time he heard my voice.

"So what do you think about this, Dr. Karos?" Using his forceps as an extension of his fingers, he pointed to an irregular yellow mass along the lower surface of the pancreatic head. "The tumor is clearly intruding into the vessel. What- tell me- would you like to do for this strapping young man?" This last part was a 'Hobbes-ism.' Mr. Ouseley was eighty-five.

I didn't hesitate. "I wanna get this thing out."

He glanced up and our eyes met for the first time since incision. "The long-term results of pancreaticoduodenectomy for cancer of the pancreas are poor, but- as you should know- no man is an average, and resection provides the only chance for cure- so we were taught by Lord Rodney Smith." His uncanny ability to conjure up old sayings at the drop of a hat was astounding. I nodded figuring my answer had been on target. "However, this disease continues to humble us and doing less for this chap is actually doing much more. We're done here. This tumor's staying put. We'll be closing," he announced.

A technically demanding procedure had been downgraded to a routine wound closure. I stretched and surveyed the room. The circulating nurse was counting our sponges, while the scrub was sorting her instruments. I could barely make out the anesthesiologist behind the drapes and wondered if he was snoozing. With the stress level down, I thought I'd lighten the atmosphere with a topic I might actually know more about. "So have you ever been to Greece, Dr. Hobbes?"

"I don't get out very much."

"Oh," I said wishing I could take it back.

"Most recently, I was there three- maybe four- years ago. The history and the culture of your ancestors are utterly fascinating."

"Even now, it's a fantastic place," I said. "It's a relatively poor country, but with wealthy people, and I don't mean everyone's affluent. I mean- the Greeks- well, they know how to enjoy life."

"Certainly," he said.

"I've seen both perspectives," I said, "since I'm both Greek and American. This country's very rich, very powerful, but for some reason, everyone's working so hard all the time, sometimes just to get by and make ends meet."

"You know," he said in a more solemn tone, "it was a Greek-Alexander of Macedon- who said, 'I am indebted to my father for living, but to my teacher for living well.' One story goes like this…"

"Yes, sir," I said while suctioning out warm irrigation fluid from the open abdomen.

"Young Alexander had conquered the then civilized world and was visiting the philosopher Diogenes who was lying in a field enjoying some leisure-time. Alexander had great respect for the philosopher and asked him what he could do for him for all of his judicious advice through the years- this as he stood over the philosopher with his massive armies battle-ready behind him." Dr. Hobbes shook his head, "No, no, no. Here. Cut here."

"Sorry."

"'I can give you whatever you desire,' Alexander told the philosopher. Diogenes didn't have to think very long. He answered, 'Well, what I would ask of you is… could you please just stand a little over and away from my sun?'" Dr. Hobbes' eyes widened, the balance of his countenance tucked away behind his mask. "You see Diogenes held firm to the belief that it's a blessing to possess what one wishes, but, greater still, not to desire what one does not possess."

I knew this to be true long before I heard it in the operating room that summer morning. Nonetheless, I felt a tacit reassurance- one of my core beliefs was being validated- hearing this maxim coming from Dr. Hobbes.

"Mr. Ouseley's voyage is ending," Dr. Hobbes said. "There's nothing either of us can do with our tools to make it otherwise. All we can hope for is that between now and the end, he will find the calm, and if what he coveted was a satisfying- but not limitless- journey, he will hopefully be able to do just that." Dr. Hobbes leaned over to the scrub nurse: "Get us the number one, double-looped suture. When you have it ready, hand it to my assistant." He turned and took a few steps away from the O.R. table, stretching his shoulders and back before returning to the sterile field. With his gloved hands, he covered my own, which I had been resting on the patient's exposed lower abdomen. "Dr. Karos, are *you* enjoying the journey?"

The scrub nurse handed each of us a pair of forceps. She handed me the needle driver with the suture needle loaded and passed a malleable retractor to Dr. Hobbes to protect the underlying bowel during the closure. Dr. Hobbes gently placed his instruments back down on the operative field. I had taken too long too answer.

"Every so often, stop and think about where you are and what it is you're doing," he said.

The scrub nurse reached over to retrieve the idle instruments. My first instinct was that I had done something wrong.

"Look around and try to measure your place in time, your achievements," he said. "Confirm *for you* that this is what you wish from life." Dr. Hobbes glanced at the scrub who momentarily had her back to us, then at the anesthesiologist who was fiddling with his machine. Leaning in, he dropped his voice to a whisper: "That way, you reaffirm you're content with what you're producing. If this is the case- truly- then you are succeeding for at that point in time, *you are living well*."

I started sewing the abdomen closed, grasping the thick connective tissue on either side with my forceps and bringing it together with the large curved needle and heavy suture material. "I think I understand," I said.

Dr. Hobbes resumed assisting. "Residency can be difficult- so it's easy to- but don't lose your perspective. Very few things are very important in life, Dr. Karos. These are the ones that need to be emphasized by you. Make sure to enjoy the journey or else you run the risk of waking up one day and feeling the dreadful 'R' word."

Responsibility? Rebellion? Relevance? "What is the 'R' word?"

Dr. Hobbes waited until I had re-established eye contact. "Regret," he said. "By the way, did Gorcki ever find my patient?"

****

Still in scrubs, I stumbled out of Brigham late that afternoon. The painful events that had pounded me as a teenager had also made me tougher and more resilient. Although I had viewed my bout of depression as a weakness during college, after battling and beating it, I gained something from all the hurt- an inner strength. Given the nature of my profession, this advantage proved to be significant. Long hours peppered with the pain and sadness of the less fortunate were my daily norm. Death was common, and although watching families grieve could be difficult, I was good at it.

My mother had provided me with the most profound food-for-thought. It was not death that frightened her but rather dying. No one deserved a painful, drawn-out end of life. In my experience, it happened all too frequently- families unable to let go of loved ones despite the medical futility making erroneous decisions which prolonged inevitable outcomes. Often, they were misled by an excess of love- the greatest irony. Dr. Hobbes' patient would eventually succumb to his disease. I hoped that months from now he would pass with dignity at his own home in his own bed with the handful of individuals he loved most keeping vigil.

My black Toyota Camry was parked on a side-street two blocks away directly in front of a children's playground. I turned on the engine and adjusted the tuner. A Bee Gees song was playing- a popular one I hadn't heard in years. I listened and was instantly jettisoned back to the summer of '87. I upped the volume until the car vibrated and shouted what lyrics I knew pounding on the dashboard with both hands.

"This is why people use drugs," I mumbled to myself.

I watched as a little boy- three or four years old- ran towards the playground gate. He took little steps bobbing up and down one side of his body pulling ahead of the other. Not far behind, his mother was in pursuit guiding a maroon stroller with large wheels. As the boy approached the sidewalk, she jogged after him cutting off his path with the stroller. He looked up at her wide-eyed with a big smile before darting in the opposite direction leading his mother back into the park where he stopped to admire the sandlot. My own mother had chased after me in a park similar to this one. A happy childhood is the closest thing to a rational man's heaven. That sense of immortality- albeit false- is a fleeting gift. If only I could have packaged and preserved it through my own life.

I reached into my bag looking for something to write on. My thoughts ran ahead, while my pen tried to keep pace. I couldn't remember the last time I had felt the urge. I looked up at the mother and her toddler as I scribbled on the page. It began to take form. A few more phrases. Some scribbles. A different word. I read it out loud editing some more as I went along. Three quarters of an hour passed. I re-wrote it on a fresh sheet and added a title- *Envious of Youth*. It read well my first poem in years.

Satiated, I sighed following the release and stepped out of the car to stretch. By this time, the mother- a thin brunette with short hair and trendy sunglasses- had placed her child back in the stroller and was leaving the park. As she passed me, I noticed an M.D. identification card hanging from around her neck.

"Ty?" she said.

I strained to get a better look through her thick glasses.

"You don't remember me, do you?" she said.

"Where do I know you from?" Her ID read 'Calliope.'

"Picture me with long, curly black hair down to my butt, a lot more make-up, no stroller."

Nothing.

"How 'bout if I take my sunglasses off," she said, "and told you how much I missed sitting on the beach on a Greek island."

"Kelly!" I said. "What are you doing in New York?"

"I just started- nephrology fellowship."

"Welcome! Third-year surgery," I said pointing to myself. "And this is your little one?"

"This is Nicholas," she said patting his head. "I'm married almost four years. We live right there." She pointed to a blue awning.

"Tell me, how's Miranda?" I said.

Kelly smiled. My face got warm. "Miranda's good."

"Where is she now?"

"She's in D.C., loving it down there."

"What's this about? Both of you were west coast girls."

"The world's small," she said. "We'll be back in California sooner or later. I'm sure this is temporary for both of us." Her smile faded. "Miranda moved a little after her mom died- lung cancer," she said nodding her head.

I remembered how heavily Maria smoked that day on the yacht. "Is Miranda married?"

Kelly showed me that sly smile again. "No, not married."

"And what's she doing in D.C.?"

"She lives in Georgetown. M.B.A.," she said. "Miranda's a smart girl."

"No question."

"She's coming up to stay with me the first weekend in October," Kelly said. "Ty, it's so great to see you, but I gotta run. I'm sure I'll be bumping into you quite a bit around the hospital."

****

Dr. Hobbes' secretary asked me to wait in his private office. A brown leather couch paired with a carved oval coffee table sat in front of two large display bookcases overflowing with medical textbooks, journals, reference books, and manuscripts. The office belonged in an English country manor not a city hospital in New York. On the other side of the room, a laptop and desktop computers flanked an untidy stack of papers cluttering the surface of his enormous desk. A mini CD player was on the floor whispering classical music. Diplomas- eight in total- resting on black matting and framed with a cherry lacquer finish were symmetrically positioned on the wall behind his leather office chair, while two other certificates- off to one side- shouted 'Best Doctor in New York' and 'Top Surgeon.' Two large framed prints- one with the Hippocratic Oath in a freestyle script, the other a signed Warhol Marilyn- covered what remained of wall space.

A side table was flooded with photographs in all shapes and sizes- Hobbes standing in front of a palm tree in a warm place, Hobbes in some sort of traditional African garb, Hobbes flanked by five men- all wearing tuxedos and toasting oversized wine-glasses, Hobbes with Mayor Giuliani, Hobbes with an intoxicated smile lying on a bed of pillows in a gondola. From where I sat stiffly on the couch, I noticed a cut-out of a comic strip hanging with tape from the side of his desktop. It depicted a gardening hoe and a dog calling each other 'bitch' and 'ho'. This was no kink in his armor. I nodded my approval and nestled my back into the leather.

"Karos, don't you have any work you should be doing." Dr. Hobbes walked in wearing his white coat over green scrubs.

"I just wanted to thank you for the other day," I said straightening my posture.

"Unnecessary. Appreciated, but unnecessary." Dr. Hobbes dropped into his chair and flung off his O.R. cap. "Is that all?"

"That's all."

"Well, no reason to waste your trip. I have a minute- maybe even two." He leaned back and folded his arms. "Tell me about yourself, Dr. Karos. Do you have a family?"

"No, I'm single," I said, "by choice."

"I should hope the choice would be your own and that you wouldn't be the victim of a pre-arranged zug-zug."

"I'm very picky- in general," I said. "It's sort of hard to find someone who, well, from the very beginning to the very end, is herself. I've reached the point where I just wanna be with someone who's a real person."

"Have you tried the airport?" His accent added gravity to the query.

"The airport?"

"I'll tell you, some of the most interesting women in the entire world are at the airport, and I'm not referring to the domestic terminal in Incest, West Virginia. I'm talking about the international stations and flights- especially in business."

"I never thought about it."

"Absolutely. These ladies are the curious ones, fascinated by the world, wishing to experience it firsthand- not through TV. They're sophisticated, speak more than just one language. They're the ones who hoped the centennial Olympiad would be in Athens not Atlanta." His eyes grew wide. "Do you know I once left for a meeting in Bristol, changed my plans mid-flight after meeting the most interesting people- men and women both- and wound up connecting to Firenze for four long nights and a half-day."

"I wish I could do something like that, but- as you know- I unfortunately don't have very much in the way of free time."

"Dr. Karos, there is always free time- whether you're a janitor, a surgeon, or the President. There has to be, and where you think there isn't, it's your responsibility to create it, to make this time for yourself. Your responsibility! Otherwise, your health suffers, your mind suffers, and- worst of all- you lose perspective for the journey. I know we spoke about this." I nodded. "Arranging to have dinner at a café in Paris with fine wine and close friends, enjoying stimulating conversation, should not be categorized as unattainable fantasy world. Never place limits on yourself, Dr. Karos. Others will try to throughout your life. You will only lose if you limit yourself."

"Agreed."

I found it difficult to lock eyes with Dr. Hobbes for more than a second so I scanned the book titles on the shelves. And there it was- a paperback translation of Lucretius' book. I instinctively sucked a deep breath in through pursed lips to mask any trace of a smile.

"The everyday can be ve-ry con-fi-ning- no doubt," Dr. Hobbes said, "but there's a whole world outside this hospital so don't learn to think about things in only one way. Don't go about things always with the same approach. Think outside the narrow cubicle." He pointed his finger at me. "My goal is not merely to teach you how to be a good, successful surgeon. There are more than enough well-qualified people around this institution to fulfill that role. I hope to teach you how to be a successful individual *in your life*."

****

My older brother Philip and I lived in a high-rise condo on the West Side. It was our parents' New York City apartment before their move to Europe. We had no choice in the union- rents were too high for either one of us to venture out alone.

After I got home that evening, I darted to my room. My bedroom hadn't changed much since high school- a single bed, a wooden desk, a flimsy office chair, and a tall, narrow bookcase half-filled with comic books. Only the worn medical texts along the upper shelves suggested change.

From the bottom drawer of my desk, I pulled out my great-uncle's komboloi and a red folder. Inside the pocket was a sheet of old-school loose-leaf with a hand-written list numbered one through ten. The paper had yellowing edges and torn corners and a crescent-shaped coffee stain blemished the lower-half. I reached for a pen and added a rule. *11. Never lose perspective for what matters.*

I stared down at the page. Dr. Hobbes had reminded me to examine my world. It had been years, but I was ready to think again. It was time to complete my list.

Chapter 3

I left the internist's office fixated on the time frame before my next hepatitis test. Forty-two days and nights of waiting felt intolerable.

When I got home, I found Philip sitting on the living room couch. His wavy brown hair covered much of his face, while his trademark baggy jeans and T-shirt concealed an overweight frame. Philip was an artist, three years older than me, with little stress in his life beyond the opening night jitters of a gallery exhibition of his work.

Maybe he saw something in my eyes? "What's wrong?"

I sat next to him on the couch and spent the next ten minutes going over the lab results and explaining to him the implications of seroconversion- the possibility of liver failure, the increased risk of liver cancer, the potential to pass infection to future partners and the consequences with respect to marriage and children. Philip listened intently and uncharacteristically did not interrupt.

"Phil, I can't take the not knowing. I can't. I can't." I dropped my head in defeat. No simple tears, but instead a heavy, choking sob.

I had managed to shake him up. "Ty, I'm here for you. Anything. I'm here for you," he said. "No, really, I mean it. If something bad happens, the Karos brothers stick together. Got it?"

I nodded.

"I mean it, knucklehead. I'm here for you." Philip leaned in for a guy-to-guy hug. Although we had grown closer over the last few years, having my brother comforting me seemed misplaced.

In the end, it was a satisfying meltdown. I felt a little better afterwards but certainly no cure. My depression- idle for so long- had been awakened, and I worried it was only a matter of time before it would once again be dictating my thoughts and actions.

****

Taking time off wasn't an option. Although patients' health was our primary focus as residents, we all too frequently ignored our own well-being. Usually, we were deeply immersed in our daily work-related activities. We kept mum about personal issues concerned with what others might think: surgical residents who complained or who took days off from work for any reason were considered weak. Duties still needed to get done and trickled down to another resident's lap. In as small a place as a big hospital, word gets out quickly if you're not pulling your own weight.

After morning rounds, I asked Ted to sign and stamp a blank prescription. I was prepared with a lame excuse, but he trusted me enough not to ask. I filled in the generic for the anti-depressant I had used during my last bout. Although newer drugs had since reached market, this particular mood stabilizer had worked well for me. The simple reassurance of having it available- even for its placebo effect- was worth the effort.

Following two hernia repairs which ran into the early afternoon, Dr. Hobbes' secretary sent me a page summoning me to his office. Although I trusted him, I held off on mentioning my exposure.

Sitting at his desk in a tailored suit, Dr. Hobbes was to the point: "Ouseley died."

"That quickly? We just sent him out. What happened?"

"Unclear. His wife told me he passed in his sleep."

"At least he wasn't in pain," I said. "Sad- knowing that someone we just took care of... He probably only had a few months, but I guess he could have spent it with family." Looking up from where I had been scanning the crevices in the floor, I saw Dr. Hobbes staring at his computer monitor. "Puts things into perspective-," I said, "what's important, what's not as important, sort of what you were saying the other day."

I hid it as best I could. My jaw quietly trembled, the melancholia seeping through my veins.

"Well, Dr. Karos, do you think it's possible that life conceals some sort of 'good' within death in the hope that we make the best and the most of our present experience."

"I don't think there's any good or bad *in* death. I don't think it matters once you're gone," I said. "Death's annihilation."

Dr. Hobbes looked away from the screen and locked eyes with me. A long second passed as he studied my conviction. He released the mouse. "You don't believe the soul can continue on?"

"How? Your soul's intertwined with your body. Your soul dies with you." I leaned forward on the couch interlocking my fingers and resting my elbows on my knees.

"And what of those individuals who believe in an afterlife. Are they misguided? Delusional?" Dr. Hobbes said. "Are all the popular world religions wrong? If so, somebody's gonna have some explaining to do."

"I think believing in an afterlife is a bad thing for two reasons," I said. "People who look forward to it as a 'better place' don't live as well as they could in the present. They don't do some of the right things *now*, and they don't *care* as much about the present, their circumstances in the present, the people in the present. Because in the back of their minds, this world just isn't as important as the next one, and yeah, I think that's a problem." I tried as best I could to keep my tone pleasant and mild so as not to sound as if I were lecturing my own professor. However, I had spent considerable time thinking about this and had clear ideas at hand.

"Go on."

I remembered I had a second point. "Also, those people who believe in an afterlife but who are afraid of what might happen to them once they get there- like the possibility of going to hell or limbo or whatever- they become so fixated on the possibility for 'later badness' that they end up not living well in the present. They're living in fear."

Dr. Hobbes began swaying forward and back on his chair. "You know the unknown is always mutually involved with hope," he said. "This allows us to cope with- even possibly overcome- our fear of death."

"If…"

"Let me play devil's advocate-," he interrupted, "a role by the way I've previously auditioned for." He pointed to the photograph of him in the gondola. "The lady who took this was an Italian senator- both of us innocent victims of an '85 Barolo." He winked at me. "Dr. Karos, if no one believed there was anything beyond this lifetime, don't you think there would be utter chaos? Even if all the religions of the world *are* wrong, and death is *finality*, maybe, maybe this erroneous belief somehow preserves order and in its own way peace of mind."

"Should we be orderly based on a lie?" I said.

"Remind me to send you some of that Barolo for Christmas. Better yet, a sixty-minute Swedish at the Sagamore might do you some good." He sighed. "I agree that religions through history have tended to be…let's use the word unreliable. Twenty-five hundred years ago, the Egyptians believed in the pharaohs, then the Greeks had their twelve gods of Olympus, then the Romans came along with their own set of deities. All this we deem today to be mythology."

"Fairy tales."

Dr. Hobbes ignored me. "In the present, we have Christians of all denominations. We have Muslims. We have Jews- my personal favorites. We have Buddhists and Hindus and many others. In another two millennia, I guarantee you many of these religions will be the mythologies of our successors. Bet you weren't expecting a history lesson, although you can thank me later for that little nugget."

"So you agree," I said. "Traditional religion is just something that's made up by us because we have difficulty accepting death as finality as you put it."

"To a point," Dr. Hobbes said. "Religions always become outdated as we learn more about our environment, as we continue to evolve. Even now, you can see how this is true. For example, 'Keep the Sabbath holy.' Well that just has less and less application in this day and age. What would happen if everyone stood still one day every week? Should doctors stop treating the sick? Should we cancel all airline flights? Shut down all restaurants? No more brunch!" Dr. Hobbes added raising his eyebrows twice. "Some of these ideas have lost meaning. Religions must update as we learn more. Outdated entities get left behind."

"They die off."

"Religions need leaders who keep current, who update the faith, who reach out to the young," Dr. Hobbes said. "These leaders must be accepting of *all* the youth with *all* their odd novelties. A religion must be malleable. It's like surgery. Twenty years ago, we would have taken out that tumor. *Now* we know it wouldn't have changed anything. I have revised my practice based on new data, new developments, new evidence!"

"That makes sense," I said.

"But most religions are afraid of change," Dr. Hobbes said. "They hinder it. And because of this, they eventually die off leaving the future ripe for new thought, new theory, and new religion."

"My line of thinking doesn't change with time," I said. "It's sort of a religion based not only on science, but also on what we know to be true and on what we *sense* as we go about our day and frankly on *reality*. This is what there is, and once you die, you die."

"But again, you forget why religion exists in the first place," Dr. Hobbes said. "Religion is necessary for the human mind. Is a lifetime all that we have allotted to us? If so, do you not find that to be a sad state of affairs?"

"Maybe, but a realistic state," I said. "And *how I think* is something you can sort of extrapolate across generations. It applied two thousand years ago in ancient Greece. It applies now. And it'll apply two thousand years from now. There's no data- there probably will never be any data- to suggest death isn't the end of you. And about what you said earlier that there might be chaos- well, I mean, there already is. The world's broken- people starving to death, people constantly killing each other for the dumbest reasons."

I felt sweat on my forehead. My heart was pounding. Dr. Hobbes was scratching a stain from his tie.

"All religions want their members to be at least a little afraid of something so they can control us," I said. "And all the superstition they spew out accomplishes is to create more chaos. People constantly fighting in the name of this religion or that religion. Probably no one's got it right, but definitely everyone's lost perspective. We're all in this together. We should be if we're not. I don't know if believing in God- any god- is a good thing. I guess that makes me an enemy of traditional religion. I think it might be better just to believe in each other. We're all here without a purpose- no strings attached- so get over it, enjoy your life and be compassionate to people and hopefully they'll pay it back."

I let a deep breath out. The melancholia was unrelenting, poisoning my organs. In the silence that followed, my mind drifted back to my most troubling question as a child: why is there anything at all?

Dr. Hobbes stared at me with a smirk on his face. I figured I was done talking. I readied myself to be taken down. "I enjoy listening to your insights, Dr. Karos," he said, "but my concern is that once you become overly passionate about a line of thinking such as your own, it's difficult going back. It's easy transitioning to a view of the world based solely on science and atheism and what we *know* to be true, but it's very hard to regain belief in- shall we say- a greater being." He sat up resting both arms on his desk, his grin wiped off. "I have this to say to you: Be wary. There is a certain hopelessness in your beliefs. You may suppose you're happier thinking in this manner now that you're young and healthy, but when you're gray and sick and death comes knocking, I'm afraid the hopelessness inherent in your line of thought may be overwhelming and may just rip you apart from the inside out."

****

I sat alone in my apartment later that night. In the darkness, my key chain had begun to resemble a hairy spider. Three dozen empty wrappers of surgical materials littered the floor, while silk and braided sutures and ties were spread out over the coffee table.

The latest strand ran out of my left hand over my left index finger, looped around the circular body of the key chain and settled between my right thumb and index finger. I raised my right hand over my left and used my left index finger to slide the strand and loop it underneath the other end before applying gentle two-handed tension to the hitch. I twisted the strand again- this time in the opposite direction- within my left hand, crossed my right hand over the left, looping one strand around the other with my left middle finger. I pulled the strands apart completing a single, one-handed square knot.

As I dropped knot after knot after knot- just over a second elapsing for each- I was reminded that a pleasurable life needn't be elusive. My own personal harmony relied on simple little things most of which came complimentary. Those things that made me smile, those things that made me comfortable, those things that kept me free of stress were all within my reach.

A sliver of city light wandered in from between the curtains. I shut my eyes and kept at it. The knots were dropping faster than my eyes could dissect the motions anyhow. Once every minute, I heard the 'kittens' cry'- friction between two strands as tension is applied- and made subtle adjustments to correct the motion preventing the material from weakening. I was getting over twenty-five square knots from each suture. When I reached the limits on a strand, I opened another, looped the string through the key chain, and started over.

My hands and fingers worked furiously, but my breathing was deep, controlled. My heart rate felt slow. Raw, repetitive activity was protective- Uncle Timos had taught me this. Like meditation, it was insulating to stress. It was the reason those freaky women were knitting during the gruesome decapitations in eighteenth century France. It was the reason the komboloi had maintained its popularity into the modern day.

I heard the front door unlock. Philip flipped the light switch and gave me a funny look. "What're you doin'?" My eyes adjusted as the bare white walls and leather furniture of the living room came into focus.

"Watching TV," I said reaching for the remote and turning on the indestructible Zenith.

"You know what I mean," Philip said shutting the door.

"Tying knots."

"Yeah, I know. Shouldn't you know how to do that by now?"

"I know how to do it. I'm just tryin' to get faster. You gotta be able to tie quickly- with one hand only, then the other, sometimes with both." I threw down the knots while alternating hands.

"That's pretty quick," Philip said. "So do you remember our phone conversation from the other night. You fell asleep talking to me on the phone."

"No, I didn't."

"I was telling you something about my day and you suddenly- out of the blue- said 'please turn down the I.V. fluids.' I said 'what?' and you sort of realized it and said 'uhhhhmmm, nothing.'"

"That didn't happen." I stopped tying. "Did that really happen?"

"Yup."

I smiled. "You know my hours."

Philip sat next to me on the couch and watched as I ripped open another wrapper. "All the sick people- the dying- doesn't it get to you? You wanna *catch* people who're on their way out or something... by cutting them open?"

"Maybe."

"Do you have something to prove to somebody? Mom and dad? Didn't get enough attention as a child?"

"It's nice to have *you* back," I said. "Maybe- just maybe- I have something to prove to myself. I wanna get real good at something- you know, something that improves me- rather than spend my time watching successful people on TV - actors and basketball players- doin' what they love for lots of money and cheering them on like I'm mesmerized by them or something. Hey, they should be watching me."

"Gimme a break! You're not as cocky as you're trying to sound." Philip got up and walked out. He came back in a minute later and flung a dress shirt at me. It landed on my head covering my face. "Hey Betsy Ross, since you're doing all this sewing, why don't you stitch this button back on my shirt?"

****

I woke up and looked over at the neon light on my night stand: five o'clock in the morning. I felt nauseated. Instantly, I threw off my covers and sat up on the side of the bed. I retched once but nothing came up. Lunging forward, I opened the bottom drawer of my desk and blindly felt around for my medication. I popped open the bottle and dropped a tablet into my palm then went to the kitchen and swallowed it whole with a sip of water.

I returned to bed and sat cross-legged with the lights off. I had done everything right the last few years. Although depression had been the impetus to my conception of the rules, their guidance had placed me on a successful path- the path leading to a tranquil mind. Having accepted that at death I will cease had given me the incentive to live. But now my fears had resurfaced. A second major wave was percolating. No one experiences only one. The first time around, I was able to convince myself of a simple truth- that the physical manifestations were fraudulent, psychosomatic. This time, the game had changed. If I seroconverted, my liver would be damaged and this couldn't be helped by adhering to any set of rules.

I turned on my desk-lamp. Despite my best efforts, pain would be present in my life. This- I knew- couldn't be the case after I died since pain only affects the living. My efforts to avoid it any way I could were central to my well-being and an inherently natural human response. To remind myself that the end did have some good mixed in, I pruned my thoughts and scribbled the next addition: *12. Life can hurt; death is painless.* The state of death is painless for sure, although the same couldn't be said for the process.

Although there was no sign of daylight yet, my nausea was gone. What did I need to do in my life to make things better? My heartbeat implied there was still time to effect change. Something was missing from my life- in fact someone. Miranda hadn't accompanied me for over a decade, but she was always inside me. The road I followed into adulthood had been influenced by the early powerful emotions she had released within me.

I stared down at the rules. Certainly they had helped me regain my strength and confidence but at the expense of something else. What was lacking was something I had left behind in an earlier time, something I had valued tremendously at a younger age- passion.

The fear of a foreign virus multiplying inside my body had changed me. Reminded of my vulnerability, I felt a new strength, an unfamiliar courage. Depression had pushed me away from Miranda, and I never accepted how much she might have fostered my timely healing. This time, the rules alone couldn't bail me out. My salvation lay intertwined with an individual. I had pinpointed what was missing from my life. The passion I longed to rediscover was specific. It was for a woman. I needed to find my little Miranda.

Tum...Fshhhhhhhhhhhhhhhh

Tum...Fshhhhhhhhhhhhhhhh

Tum...Fshhhhhhhhhhhhhhhh

"Dr. K. Dr. K. Can you open your eyes for me? OPEN YOUR EYES."

Tum...Fshhhhhhhhhhhhhhhh

"Good morning. There you go. Good morning. You're doing great. You're doing very well. Keep it up. Everything looks pretty good."

Tum...Fshhhhhhhhhhhhhhhh

"Do you want to tell me something? Yes? Yes or no? Do you want to ask me something? I know it's hard. I know it's difficult. Do you want to write it down? No? No?"

Tum...Fshhhhhhhhhhhhhhhh

"OK. Alright. You're doing great. I'll see you a bit later."

Tum...Fshhhhhhhhhhhhhhhh

Tum...Fshhhhhhhhhhhhhhhh

Tum...Fshhhhhhhhhhhhhhhh

I'm alive.

Part II

Eleven years earlier

Chapter 4

Mykonos, 1987

Under a blistering midday sun, my best friend Rob and I arrived at the port of Mykonos. As our ferryboat docked, dozens of locals were waiting hoping to lure tourists to cheap hotels or camping sites all across the island. They crowded us, frantically shouting superlatives about their lodgings, some distributing fliers moistened by the sweat on their palms. After negotiating briefly in English, we followed an elderly Greek couple holding up a 'Rooms To Let' sign into a beat-up Datsun. They had assured us their 'rooms' were in the main town where I wanted us to stay, but as we zigzagged up into the hills through winding, unpaved roads, I figured we had been duped.

With dry hot air streaming in through four open windows, Rob and I sat in the back seat looking out at the whitewashed homes with their wooden shutters and doors alternating blue, green and red. The contrast between islanders and the rowdy, skin-obsessed foreigners was glaring. The locals were returning from the market groceries in hand or from fishing boats with the day's catch preparing to join family for lunch before the afternoon siesta. The invaders were leisurely putting away their coffees, eggs and sausages and powering up rented motorbikes for the trek to yet another of the unique beaches. For visitors to Mykonos, the sun is king and a brown hide conveys a fitting worship.

"We'll put them in the back room," said the old man in Greek as we approached one of a dozen beach towns. His affable wife, noticeably resigned to subordinate status, replied in Greek, "But the paint still smells." "Χεσ' τους," the man said, which translates loosely as 'screw 'em.' Although fluent in the language of my ancestors, I kept quiet. I didn't much care. The room was merely for sleep. Not appearing Greek and having been raised in the States, I had no accent and few recognized my heritage. Meanwhile Rob was as American as a Nathan's hotdog wearing his Magic Johnson high tops in the hundred degree heat.

Rob was one of the more popular guys at our Manhattan high school- good-looking, athletic, and funny. "Respect your friends and treat them well," my parents used to say to us growing up, and I was excited to show Rob a good time in Greece before senior year. My family devotedly visited Greece every summer, but this trip was unique. At seventeen, Rob and I were both traveling alone for the first time. Our parents had been generous enough to fund the excursion, but only after we had succeeded in maintaining a 3.5 G.P.A. through the crucial junior year. Greece in the late eighties was cheap, but we had to stick to a budget and planned the three week trip around an allowance of about fifteen hundred dollars apiece.

As we got out of the car, I spotted a sign that read 'Superparadise.' Rob wasn't happy when I told him this was a gay, nudist beach: "If I get raped here, I'm gonna be pretty pissed." His homophobia settled down after I assured him there'd be just as many fully nude straight women.

The odor of fresh paint wasn't too bad. A miniature nightstand separated two single beds. Except for three Orthodox icons and a framed black and white photo of an old villager with a straw hat and a bushy white moustache, the walls were bare. The bathroom was common and in the hallway.

Rob and I emptied our bags and changed into swim trunks. We spent the next few hours baking on the sand, dipping into the salty turquoise water every half-hour to cool off. The beach was packed. Nudists and gays were concentrated over to the right side. We sat on the left where mostly singles and some families were gathered. The fatigue of the early morning wake-up and boat trip caught up with us, and we decided to forgo the main town that night. An English-speaking tourist told us about a beach party at Superparadise, and we agreed to drop by there instead.

****

The sky was alive with vivid stars and an intense full moon surrounded by a bright halo. The wind had died down, and the water was tranquil, oscillating subtly upon the shore in diminutive, serial bursts. Most of the activity was centered over a cramped, wooden dance floor and an adjacent bar while smaller patches of revelers were scattered across the beach. There were chain-smoking waifs in bikinis, horny men sipping cocktails from coconuts, and a wide assortment of tattoos, navel and nipple piercings. They had come from all over- the U.S., Canada, Australia, Japan, Brazil, and especially Western Europe. Two hundred young, uninhibited bodies lubricated in sweat- some gay, most straight, several undecided- bouncing and grinding to an animalistic beat. It was the quintessential, modern-day Greek orgy, although there were only a handful of actual Greeks.

Rob pointed with his chin. "Over there. What d'you think?" he said competing with the blaring music. At the other end of the bar, I spotted the girl- barefoot, wearing short jean shorts and a tight gray top. Her long, curly hair and thick, black eyebrows were accentuated by a purple headband with white dots and giant loop earrings.

"She's aw-right," I said.

"I'm gonna talk to her," Rob countered and walked off.

I hadn't gotten used to the freedom of being on my own. I was feeling it out in small sips, while Rob was already drunk. I followed him.

"Pardonay…pardon….uh….Sprechen zie deutsch?" he said.

The girl didn't answer.

"Parlez-vous francais?" he said.

She smiled and shook her head 'no.' Having served time in the same language class, I knew Rob's French was a disaster.

"Shit," he muttered.

"Oh, hey! Are you American?" the girl said.

I listened in. She had traveled from San Francisco and was visiting Greece with her cousin and aunt. They had arrived in Mykonos a week earlier having first spent five days in Athens. She was partly Greek but spoke only a few words. Unprompted, she told Rob she was eighteen.

"By the way, my name's Kelly."

"Robert."

They shook hands. Rob took his time letting go.

"Good to meet you, Robert. This is my cousin Miranda."

A second girl walked over and shook hands with Rob. She had dark features like her cousin but straight hair, brown eyes, and a freckled nose. Her face was perfectly symmetric. The black and white top of her two-piece concealed small breasts, while a black sarong covered her lower half.

"Rob's from New York," Kelly said.

"Ladies," Rob said, "this is my friend Ty." I smiled at both, although my heart beat a little harder when Miranda looked over at me.

The music was loud, so we huddled in. The girls were staying at a hotel in the main town with Miranda's mother. They intended to enjoy Mykonos for a couple more days then spend their final week in Athens before returning home to California. We filled them in on our plans, which included sightseeing in Athens and a visit to ancient Delphi.

"You wanna dance?" Rob blurted out of the blue. Kelly put down her drink, and we lost them as they blended in with the mob. Miranda turned her back to me, leaned over the bar and yelled something into the bartender's ear. I looked the other way out over the water. The sea had been quietly awakened by the soft, white light of the moon as it wandered across the starlit sky. Miranda handed the bartender a paper wad of Greek drachmae in exchange for an orange drink with a pink straw.

"Looks pretty tasty," I said sucking on an empty Amstel bottle.

A breeze blew in from the shore. Miranda rested her glass on the counter and put a T-shirt on. It read 'Ti amo' on the front, 'Ti odio' on the back. I only knew what the front meant. She pointed to the small print over the pocket of my own shirt, where 'University of Hawaii…KMANA-WANA-LEI-OU' had been inscribed. "Does that mean anything?"

"I think it means something in Hawaiian, but I'm not sure," I said, embarrassed she might figure it out.

"So what's Ty, Ty?"

"A couple of friends and my brother call me Ty. It's actually Timos. You have some Greek blood in you?"

"My mom's Greek. My father's Italian," she said reaching again for her drink.

"So you might've heard the name before."

"Nope."

"It's a Greek name, but it's not very common."

"I can't think of anybody with that name that I know," she said. "I'm gonna do what your friends do and call you Ty. If that's OK, Ty," she smiled.

"That's fine."

"So you're starting college next year?"

"A year from now," I said.

"And what do you want to do when you grow up, Ty?" she said sipping from the straw.

"My life's already pretty much planned out, so I can answer your question pretty specific," I said, sticking my index finger into the bottle.

"Oh really."

"Yep. Here's the plan. When I'm 24, I plan to buy my Porsche. When I'm 26, I'll have made my first million. And when I'm 28, I'll settle down and get married."

"Wow. That is pretty specific."

"I plan to have two kids- one boy and one girl, and both of them will love me much more than they'll love their mother- my son because I'll hang out with him and we'll play sports together, and my daughter, well, because girls always love their fathers more. I'm gonna be a pretty cool dad." *Slow down. Deep breath.*

Miranda turned her back again and leaned over the bar. She got on her toes, fully flexing her calf muscles. She extended more resting her body on the countertop. As her feet left the ground, her flip-flops slipped off.

A different bartender- a muscular one in his twenties wearing only a pair of shiny, black soccer shorts- came over. She spoke to him in what sounded like fluent Italian. He bent down, grabbed a pack of cigarettes and handed it to her. Miranda placed one in her mouth and leaned into his biceps to balance herself. With a lighter in one hand and the other blocking the breeze, he stroked her cheek with his fingertips as he lit her cigarette. Even with her back turned, I noticed it. He said something else in Italian to which Miranda gave him a look of disgust and dropped back down.

"Did you want one?" she said.

I watched as she slid her toes between the straps on her sandals. Her pink flip-flops perfectly matched her painted toenails. I generally avoid looking- most people have ugly feet- but hers were surprisingly perfect.

"Do you want one?" she repeated.

I panicked for a second thinking I had gotten my finger stuck in my Amstel's bottleneck then shook my head no. I considered breaking out into my anti-smoking speech but thought of Philip, who had told me many, many times how annoying I got whenever I started preaching.

"I miss my dog back in California," Miranda said. "I have a golden retriever."

"What's his name?"

"Lucky."

"I-I-I-I don't know about dogs. I think they're overrated," I said. Miranda inhaled audibly feigning a gasp. "I mean I see these people in the elevator in the city talking to their dogs. 'Now don't go Rufus, this isn't our floor.' I think they need to get a life. I mean would you allow some naked guy to sit on your couch knowing what he's just finished doing on the sidewalk? No! But it's OK if your dog does it? And to pick up after him. I mean, you've heard the joke. If aliens were watching, they'd be trying to figure out who's walking who."

"Well I live in a house not an apartment," Miranda said, staring into me until I had to look someplace else. "And we have a backyard. And my dog is very, very cool." She glanced over at the crowd reminding me with her eyes we weren't alone.

I needed to do better. I took a deep breath. "I remember," I said, "when I was maybe thirteen or fourteen we used to sit out on the porch at night with my parents when we would come over to Greece. We'd be talking, and every so often, we'd turn off all the outdoor lights and look up at the sky. The stars would be really bright, and I think I felt certain things that they didn't."

"Like what?" Miranda said. Although the cigarette sat in the middle of her mouth, she was hardly inhaling.

"I kept thinking: why is there anything? I mean what if there was just nothing at all or even beyond nothing, just oblivion?" I had learned the word 'oblivion' from the Avengers comic book. "See if there was nothing, then that would be something, right? Oblivion means that there's zero, zilch, zippo. So I guess my question is what if there was oblivion."

"You mean what if there weren't any people or any planets?" she said turning and facing me.

"Yeah, nothing at all. Absolutely nothing at all," I said. "I mean the way my parents would answer me usually had to do with religion. 'Well if there was nothing, then there would only be God,' my father would say. But that wasn't good enough. 'So who made God?'" I could tell Miranda didn't know where this was coming from. Neither did I. I just wanted to get it out of my system. "The usual answer was He's always been around, but my questioning wasn't about that. I wasn't questioning the existence of God; I went along with that. The 'why' was bothering me more than the 'who.' Why was there a God? If I tried to think too hard about it, even now, I get a jolt in my brain, sort of like hitting a dead end."

"I'm not sure what you mean by brain jolt, but I know what it feels like to search for something that always avoids you."

I nodded figuring she meant to say 'evades.'

"Don't think about it," she said. "Some of these things we never really get to figure out." Miranda placed her hand under my ribs and stroked my side up and down.

"You're eighteen? Like Kelly?"

"Do I really look eighteen? By the way, you're not the first person to ask me that," she said. "No, I'm fourteen."

****

The sky was perfectly clear. The sound of the waves spilling onto the shore was as soothing as a warm bath. The stars, the moon, and the sea peered over my shoulder as I began my free-fall.

"I had a weird dream last night," Miranda said, as we strolled along the beach a few feet from the water. "I was stranded on this island. I can't remember how I got there, but I felt really alone. This guy, sorta good-lookin' guy, appears in front of me- someone I had never seen before- and tells me to follow him to the garden. I didn't wanna go, but he insisted this garden was a beautiful place."

"What was in the garden?"

"I don't know. Let me finish," she said. "I followed him for a bit, but we were walking around in circles, and I could tell he was lost. I got really scared and just wanted to go home. Then my father came and helped me escape. I remember running over and kissing him over and over."

"That doesn't sound bad."

"I guess."

"What was in the garden?" I asked.

"My father died last year," she said.

Miranda stopped. We were fifty yards from the center of activity. Glancing down at the parched sand, she chopped at it with her bare feet again and again until a small dust cloud rose up. She had revealed a personal pain, and the beach's vast hourglass had been marked and made aware. Reflexively, I leaned in and hugged her. She responded by draping her arm over my shoulder and pressing her clenched fist against the center of my back. The tenderness in my advance faded when I felt her hand drift underneath my shirt and her fingernails scratch the skin of my lower back. She pulled me in tight pressing her small frame up against me holding me there until my arousal was palpable. Satisfied, she pushed me away with both hands.

"How often do you cry?" Miranda asked as we separated.

"Honestly, I don't think I've cried once in the last ten years. I can't even remember the last time I cried." She gave me an uneasy look. "I hope that doesn't make me a cold person or anything. It just doesn't come easy to me. I just haven't needed to."

Miranda sat down on the sand resting the side of her head on her bent knees. "You're a pretty frigid guy, Ty!"

I plopped down next to her beyond the flat rim of wet sand. "You know, you have the sweetest, sweetest voice that I have ever heard," I said. "Has anyone ever told you that?"

She smiled and let out a giggle.

"So here's a question for you that one of my teachers brought up," I said. Miranda must have sensed my own excitement, because her face lit up in anticipation. "Relevant to what I was saying before…so… if God is all-good *and* God is all-powerful, then why is there evil? Why doesn't He just make it go away if He's all-powerful? And if He's all-good, He wouldn't want there to be any evil, right?"

"I think I've heard this before," she said, "but I can't remember the answer."

"One or the other can't be the case, right? Either God's not all-good *or* He's not all-powerful," I clarified.

"Maybe things would be too easy for us if everything around us were good. I mean, there wouldn't be anything challenging us. Things would be too easy and boring. I think it gives us a choice when bad things happen to us. We can choose to react in a bad way or in a good way, but it would at least be our decision."

"That's a pretty good answer," I said.

"I mean if bad things couldn't happen to us, then we wouldn't appreciate all the good things that do happen to us."

"A really good answer."

"If you don't have the bad, then what does 'good' mean anyway? Good needs bad. And anyway, without a little badness around, Ty, I think you'd find things a bit dull." She winked at me.

"I understand what you mean," I said. "God has allowed there to be some evil, so that we decide fully on our own to, well… not engage in it. Like you said, He wants to give us the choice to be good." I leaned back burrowing my hands into the sand. "But how can you explain good people getting sick or for that matter babies, who haven't had a chance to choose to be good or bad, getting sick or suffering or dying?"

Miranda shut her eyes forcefully. "That's hard. I don't know."

"I don't know either, but it bothers me there's so much suffering around and God's not doing much about it."

None of the commotion around us distracted me from Miranda-not even a giant pelican who was randomly wandering the beach surrounded by a group of drunks. Rob and Kelly came over twice, and each time I sensed the tacit reassurance Miranda provided her older cousin. By three in the morning, Kelly was tired and ready to go. A minivan was returning to Mykonos town and the girls needed a ride back. I leaned in to give Miranda a goodnight peck on the cheek, but instead she kissed both my cheeks forcibly in a way that caused her nose to squash up against my face.

"Can we see you guys tomorrow?" I said.

"Can't tomorrow. My uncle's taking us out on his boat," Miranda said.

"All day?"

"We won't be back till late," Kelly added.

I looked at Rob. "How 'bout the day after?" he said.

"That should be fine," Kelly said. "Let's do Psarou at- say- one."

"Perfect," I said.

As they started towards the van, I whispered into Miranda's ear, "Are you bored of me yet?"

"Not just yet," she replied.

Chapter 5

The next day passed painfully slow- more static between the defining- and I retained nothing from the evening except my intense anticipation for the following day. I did make the mistake of admitting to Rob that I was interested in Miranda and was promptly labeled a child molester. This annoyed me. Fourteen was merely a number. Anyway, he didn't know her.

****

Gold sand and aquamarine water made Psarou a tourist highlight. Wooden umbrellas were planted symmetrically three rows deep and extended the length of the beach, while barren hills of moonscape flanked the small oasis. Lazy bodies lined the sand discretely checking each other out through dark sunglasses to break the monotony of staring at their own tan lines.

Miranda and I were stretched out across our beach towels, while the other two had decided to go water skiing. A charm necklace with three gold intertwined circles on a thin black leather band hung around my neck. My father bought it for me years ago after one of his long stints abroad. I was rubbing it with my fingers, as I watched Kelly rise out of the wavy sea on two skis before awkwardly flopping back in. In a teeny bikini, Miranda lay next to me- knees flexed, arms at her sides, eyes shut, facing directly into the sun.

"What're you thinkin' about?" she said moving only her lips.

I looked at all of her before answering.

"I probably think too much about things," I said.

"You analyze?"

"I do, but I wish I didn't so much. I'm pretty sure it's better just to stay busy. I spend too much time thinking about life."

"What d'you mean 'thinking about life'?" she asked.

"I mean I think the best thing that you can be in life is ambitious. Being ambitious keeps you focused on something and away from those

thoughts that lead you to all those questions you can't answer."
Miranda turned to her side before sitting up. "I mean I sometimes even
wonder if it's better to be a little dumb or self-centered to keep from
thinking about the way things are and about what the point of all *this*
is. I definitely think too much. That's why I get all melancholic."

"What's that?" she said.

The wind blew sand up into my face.

"Sad."

"Sand?"

"Sad."

"I haven't seen that at all," she said.

"I do. Trust me, I do."

We huddled in to shield our eyes but the windblown dust kept
coming. Miranda reached behind her and pulled a Snoopy towel from
her beach bag, unfolded it, and covered our upper bodies with it.

"I can hear you better," she said.

"And I can still see you just fine."

"Go on."

"Those melancholic moods- I don't have them all the time,"
I said realizing I didn't have to speak as loud. "Like if I'm working
hard with school, I won't have them. If I'm busy playing sports or just
distracted with something, chances are I won't get them. But
sometimes, they're unpredictable."

"Like when?"

"I think the feeling you get when you're melancholic affects a
similar place in your brain as when you're infatuated."

"But those two things are opposite," she said.

"But, you know, you're thinking about a girl, or in your case a
guy,"- I smiled- "that you desperately, desperately want to spend time
with. I mean this always happens at the beginning of some
relationships, and I guess only a couple of times at most."

Miranda mustered up a drawn-out "OK."

"And it usually happens to the 'love-struck' person in the
relationship when he's alone, because if he's with the girl, he has too
many other things to worry about," I said laughing at my own
observation. "Anyway, it's a fantastic place to be- the 'in love' state,
but it also lifts you into some sort of, I guess, spiritual mood that you
also find yourself in when you're looking up at the stars. At least it
does for me. And just like looking up at the stars makes you
melancholic..."

Miranda smiled.

"What?" I asked.

She laughed out loud.

"What?"

"I just want to know," she laughed even harder, "have you been smokin' crack? *What* are you talking about? You're so crazy," she said staring at my gold pendant.

"Just think about it. That part of your brain, right, that gets activated when you like someone, it becomes sort of a melting pot of emotions-good and bad. Right? You always end up frustrated or confused, or you can't make sense of the way things are. You're up and then you're down and then you're up again and then you're down again. It's impossible to control all these moods, and it's really hard to stay focused on other things. But it does make you think about things… *and life*."

Miranda grasped my pendant and began fiddling with the charm.

"Doesn't it?" I said counting the freckles on her nose. "You think about the girl and everything about her and every minute of every meeting. And you play it over in your head, moment by moment, over and over again, even trying to remember the things you said, exactly the way you said them, or the way she looked at you."

Miranda tugged on the pendant and pulled me towards her. Under the towel, our heads bumped lightly. "Like this?" she said squinting her eyes and pursing her lips.

"Because you're in this state, all this thinking makes you melancholic. Whether you know it or not or whether you like it or not, you're thinking about the way things are or the way you would want them to be and your brain's confused jumping between melancholy and… pleasure." I heard Rob's voice behind us and realized they were back from the water.

"Does this thing mean anything?" Miranda said still playing with the charm.

"I just like the way it looks."

"It's very cool." She dropped it and pinched my left nipple. "You have really small nipples, Ty."

"Well that's great. In one felt swoop, you have successfully dropped the level of conversation."

She pulled harder on it.

"Ouch. Hey!" I said.

Miranda pulled off the towel. The sun blinded me. As my eyes recovered, I saw Kelly walking with her purse in hand towards the taverna. Rob was standing over us all wet and dripping. I caught Miranda looking him over. He moved closer and started drizzling on her.

"Stop. It's cold," she pleaded, but he picked up the assault by brushing off his hair.

Miranda grabbed the side of his bathing suit and yanked on it. Rob lost his balance and almost fell on top of her. Facing each other with his body resting on the side of hers, Miranda wasn't protesting, although his wet skin must have been chilling. Rob pressed her cheeks together until her mouth puckered.

"Look at this face," Rob said. "Just look at this face. How can anyone not fall in love with this face? You are gonna break a lot of hearts in your life, Randy."

Miranda smirked through her crumpled mug but made no effort to break free. She opened and shut her lips like a fish. Rob pushed her head back against the sand. As he held her down, his forearm rested on her breast.

"Why don't you just let her go?" I said.

Rob looked at me then back down at her. "Should I let you go?"

Through her narrowed lips, Miranda mumbled, "No, this is fantastic. I'm very comfortable."

"Let her go." I grabbed his arm and pulled it off her.

"Relax, Ty. We're jokin' around," Rob said.

Miranda put her hands behind her head and yawned a smile.

"Sorry, but I think you were hurting her."

****

Later that afternoon, Rob and I packed our beach gear and said goodbye to the girls. The bus back to Superparadise was waiting and we needed to get back to shower and change for the night out. Miranda and Kelly planned to take a different bus back into town which was slated to leave a half hour after ours.

Rob and I had tickets for the late night ferryboat back to Athens. Although we had considered changing our reservation to stay a third night, we decided against it when the girls told us they might also be returning on the same boat because of a family issue on the mainland. They wouldn't know for sure until they got back to their hotel and had a chance to touch base with Miranda's mother. This uncertainty left me feeling uneasy.

As we circled around a straw fence which separated the parking lot from the beach, Rob stopped and grabbed my shirt. "Check it out." We were about forty yards from the girls, but through a break in the fence I could see that Kelly had taken off her top.

"I'm surprised," I said.

"I knew these girls were wild," Rob said. "Don't let their innocent faces fool you."

"Miranda won't do it."

"They're pretty nice, huh. I'm telling you, Kelly needs it real bad."

"Miranda won't do it."

"Bet you ten bucks she does."

"There's no way."

Miranda sat cross-legged with her back to us. She looked behind her where the buses were waiting. Reaching down for her sunglasses, she put them on and took a second look back at the fence. Our peephole was small.

"Trust me, she won't," I said.

"Trust me, she will," Rob said.

Miranda swung her right hand behind her back and, in a single motion, released the knot and stripped her top off tossing it on the towel beside her. Neither of us said a word. She lay back on her elbows and raised both legs evenly off the sand with her feet flexed like a gymnast.

"Ten bucks, buddy! I am sure Randy wouldn't mind a little bit of action either," Rob said.

"And you were calling me a child molester, you jackass."

"Ty, don't be so freakin' naïve. With that body, she's probably gone further than you have, you dumbass jackass. Now let's wait here two minutes, just two minutes, until she turns around, so we can enjoy a little bit of eye candy."

"Hey, Kelly's yours. Miranda's mine. Why don't you stare at your own woman, you stupid, dumbass, selfish jackass?"

Rob leaned in. "C'mon. We're waiting. Turn around."

"The bus is leaving. We gotta go. Let's go!"

"Just a sec."

"I'm getting on the bus," I said.

"Look."

Two guys had gone over and were talking to the girls. I couldn't tell for sure, but one looked like the muscular bartender from the first night. I watched a few seconds longer to see whether Miranda would put her top back on. She didn't.

"Rob, I'm getting on the damn bus."

****

The narrow, winding cobblestone roads of Mykonos town were tightly packed with tourists. Having already 'checked out' of our makeshift hotel, Rob and I were lugging our travel bags along the busiest of the pedestrian walkways, a wide road lined with tavernas, coffeehouses, and trendy shops selling everything from fancy jewelry to designer dresses.

Rob spotted the girls sitting on a wide stone wall directly across from the old harbor and its navy of rickety, wooden fishing boats. Deafening rap music blared from a nearby club. The girls appeared to be enjoying the tunes while watching the crowds parading by.

"I have an idea," Rob said. "Let's hide!"

I followed his lead, as we pressed up against a whitewashed building facade. We dropped our bags and slithered alongside it until we were directly behind the girls.

"I'll get Kelly. You get Miranda," Rob said.

I nodded.

We crept up to them, but as we got closer, Kelly dropped down off the wall. Rob stopped short. I pulled up behind Miranda and covered her eyes with my hands. She didn't flinch.

"I know it's you. Sono meravigliata invece che non mi hai palpato le tette," she said.

I couldn't understand a word, but it sounded sexy. As I released my hands and craned my neck around so she could see my face, Miranda forcefully pushed my arms apart, jumped off the ledge, and faced me without a hint of a smile. I felt like a child who had bothered somebody older.

Rob took Kelly by the hand and whispered something into her ear. He pulled her in the direction of the dance club and she willingly followed. Her going topless had emboldened Rob.

Miranda wore light blue jeans, a pink polo-style shirt with the collar up, and the same flip-flops she wore every day. She brushed her hair back over and over with her hands until she had captured every strand in her right fist then retracted a blue scrunchy from her wrist down and around the ponytail, stretched, twisted it, and passed it around a second time.

"We're leaving on the same boat as you guys," she said without making eye contact.

"Good. I get to see a bit more of …"

"Don't do that again."

"Sorry."

Rob and Kelly never made it into the club. Through the crowd of tourists, I spotted them violently kissing. He had her core pinned against a doorway with his pelvis, while her fingers slid in and out the back pocket of his jeans.

We regrouped and sat for a tasty dinner at a seafood taverna on the waterfront. A quarter of an hour before midnight, the bright lights of the enormous ferryboat gradually illuminated the darkness so we began our trek towards the port. Miranda's mother was already there, although we weren't introduced. She stood at a distance and didn't seem interested in meeting us avoiding all eye contact, while the girls jetted back and forth between us. The mother had booked a cabin for the three of them to rest through the overnight trip. I hoped she'd be the only one using it.

The journey back was exhausting. The ferryboat was delayed by a full hour. Although the girls had the option of sleeping on actual beds, they stayed with us in the open air near the rear of the ferryboat through the five-hour trip. Rob and I sat directly across from them on long, wooden benches. When it got cold and windy over the water, we put sweatshirts on. The girls slept head to head in fetal position for most of the trip. Rob was lying up against his duffel bag with his eyes closed, although I don't think he got a whole lot of sleep. I couldn't get comfortable shifting from one side to the other and feeling as if I were confined to an airplane seat.

I stared at Miranda as she slept hoping I would see her once more in Athens before her return to the States. She was leaving for Thessaloniki with her mother to attend the funeral of a distant relative who had died after a prolonged illness. They planned to stay there five days before returning to Athens for a single night prior to their flight back home. Kelly, meanwhile, would be flying back alone to prepare for college, and so our time with her was almost up.

As I worried about the fragile nature of our next meeting, the melancholy was settling in. I already had a pen, so I tore a bare page out of a discarded newspaper. Over the next hour and a half, as Miranda slept, I scribbled some words down. I had written a few poems in high school for class assignments. As I wrote this one, I felt the full range of up and down pass through me. I finished a few minutes before Miranda began to move around. She looked over at me, and I handed her the paper while the others slept. Miranda sat up not knowing what it was then took her time reading it. She didn't make eye contact until she had reached the end.

Thoughts in the Night

A tiny vessel of life,
So alone,
In the blackness of a moonless night.

One thousand men and women,
No two alike,
As diverse as the light passing through a prism.

Each hoping to dream a little dream.
To lie in the shade. To tan in the sun.
To play on the beach. To swim in the water.
To talk with friends. To think quietly alone.
To laugh. To shed a tear.
To find physical pleasure. To love sincerely.

To feel the joy of happiness,
To hope for the good in life,
That is the common pursuit of all!

We are all so different.
We are all so much the same.

I'll soon go back to my land.
They will soon return to theirs.
What mystery this group protects.
What a greater mystery lies inside…
Each individual player.

Yet that brown-eyed girl, who slept so tranquilly,
So peacefully, by my side….
Yes, she will remain the greatest mystery of all.

"It's not Robert Frost," I said.

"It's really, really beautiful." Miranda said these four words softly, earnestly, and with such a sweet and gentle smile that I felt as if she had kissed me.

It was dawn as our boat approached the port of Piraeus in Athens. The horizon was lit a brilliant red. The wind had died down to a light sea breeze. Miranda and I stared down at the smaller vessels in the harbor below. Rob and Kelly held hands while whispering to each other.

"I want to give you something." I removed my gold pendant with its three interlocking rings, walked behind Miranda, and clipped it around her neck. I had contemplated giving it to her ever since the moment she toyed with it. At that particular time in my life, I had little attachment to that sort of thing.

"Ty, are you sure?"

I leaned over and kissed her twice. "Cheek kisses are highly underrated. Bye, beautiful," I said and hugged her.

Rob and I started down the metal stairs, while the girls went to find Miranda's mother in her cabin. An intense sadness came over me, as we waited for the crew to permit us to disembark. The feeling persisted as I stared out the taxicab window en route to my great-uncle's home where we planned to stay for a couple of days.

Chapter 6

My great-uncle and namesake lived in London but spent his summers in Athens. With short chalky hair, kind eyes, and an ivory moustache he trimmed regularly, Uncle Timos always seemed a bit out of place to me as if he had walked out of a black and white film. He never married and although he was in his early eighties, he was active and energetic. He maintained a psychiatric practice in the U.K. but had recently begun limiting office hours.

As I saw it, Uncle Timos always appeared at opportune moments in my life. He motivated me to work hard in school- especially when my zeal was waning- by reinforcing the value of knowledge. "Take in as much as you can now that you're young," he used to say, "so you're better prepared when the challenges come. And they will come." As a young teen, I loved spending time with him, listening to stories about his life over two world wars and the political, social and cultural climates which followed. "The century of exponential human development," he would say. "Now just imagine the progress if we hadn't spent so much time killing each other." Uncle Timos had navigated through the heart of the storm with the scars and insights to prove it and for that I admired him.

His warm smile upon seeing us outside his apartment door derived from heartfelt joy. The brush of his moustache against my cheeks as he kissed me felt comforting and familiar. I could even look past his unsightly forehead scar which used to frighten me as a child.

"Come in. Come in. Come in."

He lived on the top-floor of a five story building overlooking the war museum along Queen Sophia Avenue near Athens' center. Nineteenth and twentieth century Greek paintings splashing vivid colors across the neo-classical living room walls seemed unchanged year after year, while endless volumes of books flooded an adjoining den.

"Sit. Sit," he said. "You're home now."

I was quickly reminded of the smooth, velvety texture of his crimson sofa as I eased back into it. On the coffee-table directly in front of me sat an old worn book with leather binding and thick woven pages. In gilt lettering, its title read *The Nature of the Universe*. This book was reliably in the same place as far back as I can remember. I repeated its title to myself: The Nature of the Universe. This time, I would remember it.

"I've heard a *great* deal about you, sir," Rob said staring at a Vassiliou painting. "A great deal."

I rolled my eyes. A decorated World War II veteran, my great-uncle had been a major figure in the Greek post-war political arena. Later, after completing the medical training the war had interrupted, he pursued and excelled in his first and foremost love- psychiatry. He was an accomplished and successful man. Any compliment from a child seemed misdirected and pointless.

"How was your trip, boys?" Uncle Timos' Greek was fluent, but he enjoyed English more.

"Great," I said. "We had a fantastic time... except for the boat trip back. I couldn't sleep at all. I haven't slept all night."

"You couldn't sleep? At your age?" Uncle Timos said. "You must be in love."

I felt my face flush.

"You know, Robert, your friend Timos shares my name," he said with a glimmer of pride. "Has he told you what our name means?"

"Actually, I had no idea it meant something," Rob said.

"Timos comes from the Greek word 'timios' which means honest and fair," Uncle Timos said.

"Very interesting," Rob said.

I picked up on Rob's sarcasm and stuck my tongue out at him. He came over and sat next to me on the couch.

"Then I guess 'Ty' comes from the English word 'dumbass,'" Rob whispered.

Uncle Timos slid open the drawer of a small bureau. "Timo, I have something I want to give to you."

This wasn't surprising since he always had something waiting to pass on to his namesake. Uncle Timos handed me a large komboloi. Rob looked puzzled.

"A komboloi, Robert, is a strand of one, two, sometimes three dozen beads with the tied-off end resting next to a tassel," Uncle Timos said.

I had seen this komboloi before. It had fourteen large yellow beads with a blue 'mati'- eye in Greek- hanging alongside the tassel on the knotted end. Within the Greek Orthodox faith, the 'mati' serves to ward off the evil eye- the spiteful energy generated by someone jealous or generally wishing harm. I remember my great-uncle masterfully directing the komboloi's yellow beads with his fingers. As a child, I used to take it from him and caress my own forearm and palms with the long, silky tassel.

"The strand is usually leather or a fine metal chain," my great-uncle continued. "This one is leather. The beads come in many different shapes and sizes. Some are made of ceramic, others plastic, but the good ones, like this one, are semi-precious stones."

"They're also called worry-beads," Rob chimed in.

"Much more than worry-beads," Uncle Timos said.

"No, well, I remember seeing something like this," Rob said disjointedly. "This guy on the plane was playing with one when we came over from the States. I'm sure he was nervous about flying. They're used to relieve stress, right?"

Uncle Timos took a deep breath and exhaled it slowly. He sat silent for a few seconds before continuing in a soft voice: "Komboloi are derived from komboskini- string with a series of knots used to count prayers. They were tools that provided man a way to preserve contact with God." He looked each of us in the eye. "You are correct, Robert, in that many use komboloi to relieve stress, just as during the French revolution when women furiously knitted as the guillotine came down. The thought is that performing repetitive activity protects you from stress and even mental trauma. The komboloi has a similar protective mechanism. It can help you relax and meditate, but it is also a companion and a friend. It can restore our ψυχή- our soul, Robert- to happier times in those instances when we might feel a certain loneliness."

"Who would've thought?" Rob said.

I never thought of the komboloi as an item of value. Growing up, I had the impression that it was a tacky toy peasants played with. Maybe my great-uncle knew my parents had whispered this to me and worried I had been corrupted or maybe he saw that smidge of doubt in my eyes.

"Those who speak uncaringly of it..." Uncle Timos said in a much louder voice. "Those who speak uncaringly of it," he repeated, "are the uninformed and the ignorant who don't understand the power and the history of this instrument. And in this komboloi, the history is vast. It was given to me by a fellow soldier who had been wounded by a German in '44. A friend and a deeply devout man." He sighed. "His fear of a brutal wartime death made him more and more dependent on God. This komboloi helped him dutifully pray, hoping he would survive his injuries and return to his family. He lived, but his family was killed. He gave this to me after the war. He wished for me the same strength it had provided him. And it has provided me with strength and courage for years. Timo, it will do the same for you. It will help you find what's important. It will remind you happiness must be sought and that we must be active participants in our own lives."

****

Using my great-uncle's home as our base, Rob and I spent the next three days traveling the mainland. We went to Olympia, Epidauros, and Delphi by tour-bus. I had been to each of these ancient sites when I was younger but appreciated the history much more this second time around. Still, my thoughts frequently drifted, as I replayed my interactions and conversations with Miranda over and over and over again. I figured this must be one reason some memories stick while everything else quickly becomes lost- those memories which give us pleasure we re-examine again and again until they end up defining us.

Ancient Delphi is perched on the slope of Mount Parnassus above the Gulf of Corinth. The historic site includes a temple dedicated to the god Apollo, a white marble theater, and, further up the mountain, an athletic stadium. The modern town is adjacent to the archaeological site and is littered with touristy restaurants and souvenir shops. As the sun crosses the mountains, the panorama of the valley below with its sea of olive trees is dream-like and seeing it again resurrected in me the deeply guarded certainty of my own insignificance.

The inside of the air-conditioned bus smelled like mothballs. Rob and I sat in the back row, while mostly European tourists lined the seats in front of us. The tour guide- a middle-aged Greek woman who couldn't mask her accent- alternated between English and French.

"Delphi was a revered site in ancient Greece," she said in a monotone while holding a tiny microphone up to her mouth. "Home to the oracle Pythia, a mystical woman who sucked in magical vapors that gave her the ability to foretell future events."

"Weed," Rob muttered.

"Her prophecies held great weight and they even influenced political decisions of the time," the guide said. "The nature of the prophecies was often- how you say- equivocal. One legend has it that a great king once approached the oracle for guidance prior to launching an invasion of a neighboring territory. Pythia informed the king the consequences of such a war would be the devastation of a great empire. Time would prove the oracle's prediction correct, but the celebrated empire that was wiped out would be the king's own."

Rob and I started our Delphian tour at the Castalian Spring, a small marble basin into which the mountain spring water collected after streaming through bronze spouts molded in the form of lion heads. According to the guide, it was at this site that pilgrims cleansed to purify their souls prior to visiting the oracle. Following tradition, Rob and I washed our sweaty hands and foreheads. Given the dry climate, I was surprised to see a giant rainbow appear high above us.

We climbed up to the ancient stadium as the hot rays of the sun bore down on us. Although it was built twenty-five hundred years ago and was frequented by thousands upon thousands of visitors annually, it was a well-preserved structure. It had been used to house the Pythian Games, a pan-Hellenic festival of athletic and literary events in honor of Apollo and named after the oracle's priestess. The stadium's track- now covered by dirt and weeds and surrounded by a forest of pine trees- ran the length of two modern-day football fields.

As a child, I had been a big fan of Greek mythology. I recalled some legends relating to Apollo and passed them on to Rob, who actually seemed interested. I thought up more, including some with my three favorite characters- Odysseus, Achilles, and Prometheus, and for an enjoyable half-hour, Rob and I sat in the shade of an olive tree and went over them.

"Let's race!" Rob suddenly blurted out. "The length of the field!"

"Why?"

"Do it for your athlete forefathers."

"No."

"It'll be cool. Trust me."

Rob continued to insist, and I finally gave in. We walked to one end of the stadium, put down our cameras and water bottles, and got into starting position by crouching down and placing one leg forward.

"Ready. C'mon. Let's do it for Vangelis," Rob said evoking the music from *Chariots of Fire*. We lingered another moment for a group of tourists to stroll out of our immediate path. "Ready. One more time. Ready. Set. Now!"

We kicked up a dust cloud of ancient dirt sprinting across the length of the stadium floor. Rob was ahead, but I caught up. In a matter of seconds, it was over and I had won. A short round of applause broke out from the international group of sightseers as we panted at the finish line with our hands on our hips.

Our guide spent a considerable amount of time telling us about the ομφαλός or omphalos, which literally means navel in Greek. We went there next. It was a large stone- possibly a meteorite- carved in a manner resembling a beehive. The ancients deemed it the center of the universe and believed it symbolized death and rebirth and provided a portal for communication with their divinities.

With a look of incredulity, Rob threw his arms up in the air. "I predict that as we stand here today… at the center of the universe… that this will forever mark a turning point for us." He raised his voice: "From this day forward, with Apollo as my witness, everything will change. We will embark on parallel, fulfilling quests, ambitiously pursuing excellence, beauty, and love. We will not falter. We cannot compromise. We cannot fail."

I nodded in agreement. Although I was the ultimate cynic when it came to prophecies, I got caught up in the moment: "My Pythia, I predict that many years from now when I'm an accomplished man near the end of it all, I'll be laying on my deathbed and Miranda will be next to me holding my hand, comforting me, crying a stream of tears."

Rob shook his head and started walking towards the bus. "Enough already! Give it a rest."

****

Back in Athens the following afternoon, Rob briefed Uncle Timos about Delphi, while I quietly left the living room to phone Miranda. She was happy to hear from me, and we made arrangements to meet later that evening. This was my last chance to see her. Her flight to San Francisco was leaving the next morning. Although I would have preferred to see her without Rob, I couldn't completely blow him off either. Rob knew how I felt about her, so I hoped he would give us at least a little alone time.

We went to Akrotiri, a dance club which was on the beach along the southern Athenian suburb of Vouliagmeni. Rob and I arrived a few minutes early dressed casually in jeans and button-down shirts. A large crowd of teens and twenty-somethings had already congregated behind a green velvet rope. I spotted Miranda getting out of a taxi, and we began to weave our way through the chaos to get to her.

She had barely stepped out of the back seat, when a guy who looked like a Greek Al Pacino in his prime approached her. He said something to her just as we got there. Ignoring him completely, I cut in front and kissed Miranda on each cheek. While Rob greeted her, I turned to Pacino and said in English: "Sorry, buddy. She's with me." For all I knew, he might have been someone she knew, but my gut insisted he was merely another overconfident prick.

The three of us snaked back through the crowd towards the velvet rope. The bouncer took one look at Miranda and unfastened the hook. Rob and I pushed in behind her. The club was massive with half a dozen small bars situated around an active dance floor. A mix of house and pop blared to the point that simple conversation was impossible, so we walked past the commotion to an outdoor area overlooking the water which was more subdued and much less congested.

"Catch us up, Randy," Rob said, as we settled around a wobbly metal table. "Have you done *anyone-* I mean *anything-* interesting that we should know about since the last time we saw you?"

"You mean other than the funeral," she said.

"That's right," Rob said. "Sorry."

I knew he wasn't.

"Don't worry about it," Miranda said stroking his forearm.

"My condolences," Rob said before placing his arm around her shoulders and hugging her.

Miranda rolled her eyes. "I barely knew the lady."

I watched to see whether Rob would remove his arm from around her but he kept it there.

"When someone dies," I said, "especially if it's someone we know well, don't you guys think it forces us to think about our own life?"

"Sure does," Rob said. "Hundred percent. All the time. You the man."

I ignored him. "You come across all these really troubling thoughts that are difficult to control and sort of tough to put aside," I said. "I mean with time, we get better, but not before really getting frustrated, you know, just thinking about those impossible-to-answer questions."

"Like why do men have nipples?" Rob said.

"Like why is there anything? What if there was nothing at all?" I said. "Think about it. I bet you'll get a brain jolt."

"A what?" Rob said.

Miranda leaned over and whispered something into Rob's ear. He smiled and whispered something back. I looked out over the water.

We ordered a round of cocktails. No one checked IDs. Miranda asked for a Vodka-Cranberry and finished it even before I was half way through my Screwdriver. A second round followed, and we were all getting tipsy.

Without explanation, Rob got up and walked into the club.

"So are you excited to be going back to the States?" I said.

"Not really. The summer passed too quickly," Miranda replied. "Ty, I'm just gonna run to the ladies room."

It was a warm night. There were couples walking along the beach. Tiny waves were pulsating onto the shore. I looked up at my favorite roof searching for the man in the moon, but he wasn't there. At least five or six songs went by. I looked behind me into the club to see if I could spot Rob, but there was no sign of him at the nearest bar. Pacino stepped outside with a drink in his hand, and our eyes met. He motioned to a friend, and the two of them walked over.

"Where is your sexy girlfriend?" Pacino said in broken English convinced I was a foreigner.

"She's in the bathroom," I said. "Why?"

Pacino turned to his friend and this time in Greek said, "This guy's a complete idiot." I pretended not to understand looking back and forth between them. "He's completely in his own world," he added.

"Malakas," his friend said as they proceeded towards the beach.

"What's goin' on?" Rob sat down and reached for his drink.

"What happened to you?"

"I went for a walk."

"Where?"

"Around the club. It's huge, and it's so crowded it's not easy getting around."

"Did you see Miranda?"

"I think she went to the bathroom."

Although there wasn't much light where we sat, I could see Rob's hair was disheveled. Miranda returned and took her seat. She didn't make eye contact with me.

"Where'd you go?" I said.

Miranda looked at Rob. "I was in the bathroom. There was a long line."

Fireworks suddenly broke out over the water. Miranda looked up behind her, and I noticed sand mixed in with her thick black hair. *Sand?* As the lightshow blasted overhead, club-goers poured out onto the beach. Meanwhile, the conversation at our own table had died. Rob and Miranda sat quietly, and I couldn't think of anything to say.

"I told my mom I wouldn't be late," Miranda said. And with those words, the night and my summer came to an end. We left the club and found Miranda a cab. Reluctantly, I shut the door behind her.

I stood there watching the taxi speed away. "What just happened?"

"What?" Rob said.

"Tonight. I mean what happened tonight?"

"You should've made a move," Rob said. "Ty, you're too passive. I told you these girls want action. She wanted you to make a move." Rob put his arm around my neck. "This was her last night in Greece. She wants to have a story to tell her friends when she gets back that she had a summer fling. She wanted you to make a move. I'm positive."

"She's fourteen."

"Doesn't matter. You blew it, man. She doesn't think you're interested."

Driving my Camry down I-95. Can't wait for the summer. More I think about it, faster I wanna go. Speedometer's reading 90. *Hysteria*'s on the radio. I'll open the windows. All of 'em. Wind's coming in from every direction. The music needs to be louder- to the max. Exhilirating! A little harder on the gas. What a fantastic way to die! Make my Toyota into a Porsche Carrera. Up the speed to 100, 110, then 120. Blast Def Leppard until the music drowns everything out. A high velocity motor vehicle collision. An instantaneous end. Quick and painless. No suffering.

Wait. The car's not slowing down. Brake's not working. Wait, there is no brake. Uncle Timos, put your seatbelt on. Hold on. Oh my God, we're gonna hit the wall!

Gasp. Gasp.

Tum...Fshhhhhhhhhhhhhhhh

I can't stop!

It's not stopping!

Tum...Fshhhhhhhhhhhhhhhh

I can't breathe!

Tum...Fshhhhhhhhhhhhhhhh

I can see. My eyes are open. I can see.

Tum...Fshhhhhhhhhhhhhhhh

Tum...Fshhhhhhhhhhhhhhhh

"OK. Just relax. Just relax. Here comes some happy juice. Have a nice dream. Dream of a happy place."

Chapter 7

From the twenty-third floor of our West Side condo, I looked out at the yellow night-lights of the midtown Manhattan skyline. Bits of frost lined the bottom of my bedroom window. This had been a cold February.

"What the hell are you doing?" Philip said, as my door swung wide open.

I had a fifteen pound silver dumbbell in each hand. "Working out," I said, although my brother could see that.

An aspiring artist at Parsons School of Design, Philip had his oil on canvas abstract paintings exhibited in local galleries on two occasions. Even I thought he was talented. Philip preferred living at home along with all the advantages that came with it, so he commuted to school by subway. A good guy deep down, he could effortlessly transform himself into a real pain.

"Since when do you work out and next time ask me if you're gonna use my weights," he said sitting on my bed cross-legged and barefoot in his shorts.

"Fine."

"Why're you working out?"

"Because I feel like it."

I curled each dumbbell staring at the underwhelming muscles on my skinny arms off the reflection in the window. I hoped he wouldn't see the photograph, but it was too obvious to miss. After all, I had the fantasy bedroom of a generic minimalist- desk, chair, bed, lamp, bookcase- with little in the way of clutter.

"What's this? Who's this?" Philip picked it up off the floor. "She's cute in a mousy sort of way."

"You're being an ass."

It was the only picture I had of Miranda. On the beach. Curled up in a ball. Arms wrapped around her legs. Head resting on her knees. It was her smile that made me push harder.

"Is she naked?" Philip said.

"No, it's the angle," I said. "She's got a bathing suit on."

"I think she's naked," he said. "How d'you know her?"

"From the summer."

"She lives here?"

"California."

"Have you seen her since then?"

"No."

"You haven't seen her in six months?"

"No. We write each other."

"Letters? What are you- Winston Churchill? Why not just pick up the phone?"

I dropped the dumbbells and shrugged my shoulders. "She lives across the country. It's expensive- I'm not in the mood to explain those calls."

"Even once? Who cares? Just call her. What- are you afraid to?

"No."

"Then?"

"Just forget it."

Philip tossed the photo back down on the floor. "Are you infatuated with her?"

"No."

"Well just don't fall in love with her."

"I'm not."

"Trust me. You don't wanna depend on anybody else. They'll just letcha down."

"I won't."

Philip grabbed the *Sports Illustrated* swimsuit issue from my bookcase. "You better keep working out. You got a long way to go."

The dig didn't bother me. I was genuinely inspired to improve myself. In every way. I had the best reason to.

"I'm doing this for me not for any girl," I said. "Anyway, women fall in love with what they hear not with what they see."

Philip looked up. "Oh boy, Dr. Ruth is in the house- zhi importance of zhi penetration."

I started another set.

"Mom and dad are back tomorrow," Philip said.

"I know."

My parents were hardly ever home. Born and raised in Greece, both came to New York in the late sixties for post-graduate studies and better work opportunities. Later, my father- a career diplomat- served as ambassador to Ecuador for six years. During that time, he spent almost three weeks a month away commuting back and forth to New York to see us.

"Dad's leaving again next week," Philip said.

"Where to now?"

"Athens. Setting up for the move."

My father had been appointed to the consular section of the U.S. embassy in Athens- an honor as well as an opportunity to spend more time in Greece. My parents planned a permanent move back during the upcoming summer. By the fall, Philip and I would both be in college and the prospect of returning to warmer weather was one they welcomed.

"Uncle Timos is coming on Saturday," Philip said.

"What are you- a travel agent?" I said.

"Gu-bye," Philip dropped the magazine, bounced off the bed and walked out.

I pushed on the door to make sure it was closed. From my desk, I removed a pair of hand-written letters from Miranda. I reread each one then held them up to my nose to see if they had an aroma.

Two weeks after my return to New York last summer, I had written Miranda a generic letter about my life as a high school senior at Collegiate, the all-boy Manhattan private school which I had attended since sixth grade. I mentioned how the final year wasn't stressful but that the college application process was painful and time-consuming. A month later, Miranda replied with a short letter of her own essentially detailing her flight back home and the start of her own school. I sent her a second letter, which she also replied to a few weeks later.

Letter-writing allowed me to say exactly *what* I wanted to say exactly *how* I wanted to say it. It gave me all the time in the world to work through my thoughts, collect and organize them, and arrange my words so they were perfect. No uncomfortable pauses. No shyness. A skillful control of language is power. But I also liked its romantic appeal- the personal hand-writing, the longer gaps between communication, the distance which the correspondence had to travel. I began to adore it. The only thing I loved more than writing a well-thought out letter was the thrill of receiving one from Miranda. The anticipation- not knowing what news the envelope contained- was exhilarating.

In my third letter to her, which I sent off after the new year, I included a hand-written poem.

The Moment

Be cautious not to live through your life,
Rather
Live it and to its fullest.

Be cautious not to be trapped in a mind,
Riddled
In bad and sorrowful memories.

If despair one day approaches,
Grieve as you must,
Remember
The good in life awaits your return,
As your departed now mourns for you.

A mere lifetime in forever-ness,
That is all that we have been given,
Remarkably
It is more than enough if we know how to live, day by day by day,
Restore a smile on your face and live in the moment, day by day by day.

Poems and letters. Letters and poems. I had stumbled across a natural union.

****

I sat in the living room with my father, while my mother prepared lunch in the kitchen. My father had the *New York Times* unfurled like an Olympic medalist celebrating with his nation's flag. A pair of neatly ironed beige slacks and black loafers- his traditional comfort clothes- poked from underneath the paper. "Grown men don't wear shorts," he used to tell me, although that morning I was cozy in my cottons.

"Are all his stories true?" I asked.

"They're all true," my mother yelled from the kitchen in her strong Greek accent.

"I didn't ask you. I asked dad," I yelled back. "How'd she hear me?"

My mother was wiping her hands with a cloth as she turned the corner into the living room. "Timo, I met some of these people when they used to come by his office," she said, then in Greek: "The brain has no limits into where it can reach... in good ways and in bad." She nodded twice so as to reinforce her view before drifting back into the kitchen.

I figured she was disappointed that I might be doubting her favorite uncle. "What do you think?" I said in a softer voice.

One edge of the paper folded, and my father's round, spectacled face came out of hiding. "Ehhh... your uncle puts a little 'alataki,'" he said. A little salt on top suggested an embellishment of the truth.

Uncle Timos arrived in his trademark travel outfit: a classic, pin-striped Armani suit under a Burberry trenchcoat, a pair of crocodile shoes, an auburn Stetson hat, and an elongated black umbrella which he used as a walking stick. Once he was done greeting my parents and settling his things in my bedroom, he shuffled Philip and me into the living room. Having cared for some of the most 'far gone' psychiatric patients, my uncle kept us entertained with exciting often macabre tales.

I sat next to Uncle Timos on the couch and snuck a look at the raised scar that ran from one side of his forehead to the other. It was more apparent at certain angles and downright ugly under bright light. The story behind it was one of his darkest, and Philip and I wanted to hear it again.

"Oddly enough, her name was Zoe," my great-uncle said, as he rolled back the sleeves of his purple checkered dress shirt. "Ζωή. Life!" he said forcefully. "Zoe was a patient of mine in London."

"She was bonkers! She was crazy, right?" Philip slid off the chair and onto the floor near our great-uncle's feet.

"Well, Philip, 'bonkers' and 'crazy' are not words I use to describe my patients. She had a moderate bipolar disorder- what we call manic-depressive- which was greatly worsened by the fact that she was also a substance abuser. She also had a history of violence."

"She was a drug addict, right?"

"Yes, Philip, she was. Over the course of a few months, I was helping her get off of drugs and prescription narcotics. One evening, I was in my office late getting ready to leave for the day when Zoe knocked on the door and I let her in."

"Why would you do that? You were alone that night." I asked a variation of this question every time I heard the story. "Why would you let someone like her into your office if you were alone?"

"The rest of my staff had left for the day," Uncle Timos said. "She had made such great progress under my care and despite her history of erratic behavior I honestly felt I could help her make positive changes in her life. I *trusted* Zoe."

"Big mistake," Philip chimed in.

"After I let her in, I quickly realized she was under the influence-probably heroin. She asked me for a prescription for painkillers. I said I couldn't do that for her, but I would be willing to help her with her cravings by having her admitted to the hospital and de-toxed."

"Big mistake," Philip repeated.

"She refused and then pulled the knife on me."

"And you didn't try to fight her?" Philip asked. "Did you try at all to block it?"

"No. I didn't move a muscle. I didn't even flinch as she waved the knife around." Uncle Timos pulled a silver pen out of his breast pocket and swung it slowly from side to side like a pendulum to illustrate. "I stood there motionless up until she struck me with it."

"But why? Why didn't you defend yourself?"

"Timo, I just could not make myself believe that she would do it-that Zoe would hurt me in that way. It just wouldn't register in my mind. I believed I had earned her trust and she had earned mine."

"Big mistake," Philip muttered under his breath.

"So she slashed me across the face and proceeded to stab me in the chest missing my heart by centimeters." Uncle Timos shook his head as he slid the pen back into his pocket.

"Were you afraid of dying?" I asked.

"I, for one, am not," Uncle Timos said.

"Never?" I said.

"As you enter your eighties, many friends have died," he said. "Family members have passed on. Many people you've spent your entire life with are no longer around. You're more tired, less able to care for yourself. And everything around is changing. You don't recognize the music. The movie stars you grew up with have been replaced. And the technology- I'll never understand those computers. As you get older, you begin to feel like you don't belong in this world anymore. I think it's God's way of telling us it's alright to begin letting go."

"But you don't feel like that right now," I said. "I mean you have so much energy."

"It's your fault for trusting Zoe," Philip said. "My general rule is: Don't trust anybody. Ever! People are naturally evil. People suck."

"Well I wouldn't go that far," Uncle Timos said.

"If people could be bad, they would be bad," Philip said looking over at me with a glare that said 'Trust me, not him.' "Give someone a little bit of power, and they will become bad. People who are nice are nice only because they have to be. Very few people are naturally nice because they want to be. My general rule is: Trust no one."

This attitude was typical of my brother. He was always suspicious of people's intentions. The constant cynic. Philip was simply being Philip, and his reaction wasn't surprising.

"If you continue to think in such a fashion, Philip, you'll never be happy," Uncle Timos said. "You'll always have doubts about people. You'll never be able to let yourself go, to surrender yourself to anyone."

"Maybe that's a good thing!" Philip looked back at me again and shook his head: "Trust no one."

Chapter 8

An early morning mist drifted through the red maple trees along I-91 as Rob and I approached Hartford. Trinity- one of three colleges which had accepted me- required a second look, and although Uncle Timos was only staying a week, I needed to take a day to figure things out.

I had passed my driver's test only three months earlier. My parents had been encouraging and supportive through the winter taking the time to make sure I was comfortable and safe while riding beside me on long Saturday morning trips to nowhere.

My komboloi was hanging from the rearview mirror of my parents' Honda Civic tapping on the dashboard throughout the drive up. I could tell it was annoying Rob, whose decision to tag along for company was reassuring to my mother, but I didn't much care.

We found the admissions office and were straight away directed to a tour group with eight other applicants.

"What's up with that guy- the tour guide?" Rob said. "He looks like Mr. T."

The student who was showing us around campus was Chinese and had a black mohawk, silver earrings, and a half-dozen thick gold chains around his neck. He wore a full-body, hillbilly blue jean outfit.

"More like a Mr. Tsai," Rob said.

Mr. Tsai was actually quite nice. He answered all our questions and showed us around the college grounds, including the library, the cafeteria, some classrooms, the indoor gym, and the athletic fields. He ended the tour at one of the dorm buildings. By this time, the rest of the group had broken away, and with only Rob and me still around, Mr. Tsai decided to show us his own room.

As he unlocked and pushed open his dormitory door, I immediately got a whiff of a foul smell. An exceptionally thin woman sat barefoot and cross-legged on a small futon couch smoking something illegal.

"Guys, that's my girlfriend Cybill," Mr. Tsai said.

The studio room was tiny but somehow able to accommodate the vital kitchen appliances. Worn clothes, shoes, books, and garbage were scattered across a cheap brown carpet. Cigarette butts floated in Dixie cups on a wooden coffee-table, while two columns of empty beer cans had been neatly balanced on one end. The woman looked up at us and blew smoke out her thick pouty lips. She harbored a mix of ethnicities- Japanese seemingly in the fusion- and had light brown eyes and black hair with an auburn streak in the front. Cybill wore faded blue retro shorts and an oversized Purdue sweatshirt which hung all the way down her left shoulder exposing a sleazy collarbone.

"You guys want me to read your cards?" she said in a flat tone with a subtle East Asian accent.

Rob completely ignored her. He picked up a Playboy off the floor and started leafing through it. Cybill glanced over at me.

"I'm actually not really into that stuff," I said. "It makes me a little nervous. I'd rather not know."

"Don't be a wuss," Mr. Tsai said.

"Thanks anyway," I said. "Actually I think we need to get going."

Rob sat down on the carpet leaning his back against the wall. "Go ahead. We have time," he said without looking up from the magazine.

"Listen, if you want, I don't have to tell you about things that'll happen to you," Cybill said. "Just pick a person you know."

"C'mon dude," said Mr. Tsai. "She doesn't bite, unless you stick your tongue in her…"

"Fuck you!" Cybill snapped.

"Relax! I was gonna say 'ear,'" said Mr. Tsai. He opened the door to a mini fridge adding 'dumb bitch' under his breath.

"Alright fine," I said, "but then we need to go."

"Sit," she said waddling her bottom to the edge of the futon.

I crouched down on the floor in front of her with the coffee-table between us. Cybill pushed some of the filth to one side. She looked into my eyes more than once while shuffling the deck. The cards were wider and longer than normal. I peeked at the underside as she jumbled them around. Although some had standard numbers and suits, others were filled with colorful images of castles, dragons and sorcerers. I had never seen tarot cards up close.

Cybill looked up. "Who should we talk about? Choose somebody you know, and I'll tell you about them."

Spiros G. Frangos   77

I looked around at Rob, but he was consumed by the porn. I hesitated. "OK. Tell me about the girl of my dreams."

Cybill didn't react. She cut the cards and fanned the deck across the coffee-table. "I want you to choose one."

I pointed to a card. Cybill inhaled smoke from her joint before flipping it over. The card was numbered 'XIII' and depicted a skeleton in a black hood riding a white horse. The creature had bright red eyes and held a scythe with blood dripping from its pointed end. Dead bodies and skulls were lying in the foreground.

I looked straight up at the ceiling in defeat. "You don't have to tell me what that means. That's the death card, right?"

Cybill hesitated. "No. Not necessarily. That's not what the card stands for all the time."

"What the hell does that mean?" I said with a smile trying to suppress my annoyance.

"It doesn't necessarily mean someone's gonna die," Cybill said. "Could mean that there are challenges ahead or that they're gonna be changes in your life. Or sometimes it means a difficult time will happen, but things'll get better after it's over and you'll be the better for it."

The marijuana odor was getting to me. "That's why I hate these games," I said before sneezing.

The room was quiet. No one suggested God should bless me.

"That sucks," Rob said splaying out the centerfold.

Mr. Tsai patted me on the back: "The death card, man. Your chick's toast. Wanna beer?"

****

We drove back to Manhattan later that afternoon under heavy rain. I dropped Rob off in Yorkville then made my way towards Sotheby's auction-house, where I had promised Uncle Timos and Philip I would pick them up and give them a ride home if the thundershowers persisted.

It didn't surprise me that Uncle Timos wanted to pay Sotheby's a visit. The dynamic nature of the house's activities intrigued him, and I occasionally heard him complaining about the stagnancy of museum art. He frequently took Philip and me to the premier art houses to expose us to- as he put it- works which after sale often vanish into homes never to be seen again for many years if at all.

I pulled up to the main entrance on York Avenue and saw them waiting inside beyond the revolving doors. Philip spotted the car, and they made their way towards the street with the doorman shielding Uncle Timos under a black umbrella that was more like a small tent. As he got into the car, gradually positioning himself in the front passenger seat and ever so cautiously shutting the door behind him, I was reminded of my great-uncle's advancing age. He sat with his back fully erect facing directly forward, his legs closely aligned. Had I not known this to be his customary posture, I might have thought he was uncomfortable.

"This weather blows," Philip said reclining in the back seat. "You want me to drive?"

"I'm good," I said.

I hesitated momentarily before placing the car into drive to see whether Uncle Timos would put on his seatbelt.

"Uncle," I said pointing to the strap.

He reached back but couldn't grasp it.

"Wouldn't want you to get a ticket," he said.

Philip helped him retract it forward. Uncle Timos pulled on the belt and held it halfway across his abdomen without securing it.

"Much too restrictive for an old man like me."

I drove to the 73rd Street entrance to the southbound FDR planning to get off on 53rd Street before heading cross-town. The komboloi resumed its beat interrupting the steady squeal of the wipers. I saw a brief flicker of a smile on my great-uncle's face.

"How'd the interview go?" Philip said.

"My interview was over a month ago. I just wanted to see the place one more time before I make any decisions," I said. "I'm nervous about the weather up there. Those New England winters can be really cold and snowy."

"Undoubtedly," Uncle Timos said. "And don't forget the rainy autumn. There's ample opportunity for some real soul-searching any time you mix unfavorable climate with lonely woodlands. You'll learn just as much about yourself as you will about the world around you. Great education any way you cut it."

We turned onto the FDR Drive's access ramp, and I pressed on the gas. The street was wet, but the rain had tapered off to a light drizzle.

"Have you thought about a major?" Uncle Timos said.

"Not sure," I said.

"Don't forget medicine."

I figured it was my turn. He had already given up on Philip.

"Are you really thinking about being a doctor?" my brother said. "Man, this weather sucks."

"I haven't ruled it out," I said. "It's a good life. The human body's interesting. You get to help people, and the money's not bad."

"If you wanna make money, don't go into medicine. Not anymore," Philip said. "That game's over. Maybe investment banking, but not medicine."

"You wanna be an artist. There's no money there," I said.

"I plan to do what I like."

"No one should go into medicine in the interest of making money," Uncle Timos said.

"Rob agrees with Philip," I said. "He thinks medicine's lost its luster."

Uncle Timos shook his head. "People who speak ill of medicine are fools who become aware of their foolishness only in their own hour of need."

The right lane was congested by the 64th Street exit, so I put the left blinker on and wove into the middle lane.

"Trying to convince the best and the brightest not to go into medicine because there isn't as much money as there once was is curiously self-destructive- especially in an educated society," Uncle Timos said.

"I have to agree with you on this one," Philip said. "It's like a guy on a tightrope who keeps trading in his strongest ropes for cheaper ones. Sooner or later, he's gonna end up on his head."

"Nice example," I said.

"I'm supporting you, genius. Lay off."

There was more traffic ahead. I glanced at my driver's side mirror and accelerated into the left lane.

"What do you think about tarot cards?" I said.

"Rubbish," said Uncle Timos without hesitation.

"Alright, alright," Philip said. "I know there's a pathetic story behind this one. Spill it. What happened?"

We were going about forty miles per hour. The wipers swept at full capacity when the front windshield was sprayed with a stream of rainwater by a van driving in the opposite direction. I felt a chill up my back. For a second, I lost the road completely. "Goodness," Uncle Timos exhaled. I pressed on the brakes gently and tried to keep the car steady until the wipers could catch up. A large bang emanated from the right rear. The force propelled us to the left and a second thud followed as our Civic collided with the Jersey barrier, jettisoned forward, and began to spin counterclockwise.

Although it happened instantaneously, events seemed to be unfolding in slow motion. The window-wipers erased the pool of dirty rainwater giving me a clear view of the opposite lanes and the river beyond. As our car continued to skid, the friction of rubber with asphalt created a blaring screech. I overcame the inertia just enough to glance at my great-uncle and be horrified at the site of the bulging metal bumper of the SUV in front of us approaching quickly and then pummeling into the passenger-side door. My jaw struck my shoulder as Uncle Timos and I were thrust over to our right. My final recollection was my great-uncle's gentle, peaceful countenance as his silver head of hair burrowed through the window.

Chapter 9

The screaming sirens of an ambulance. *Strange?* They weren't getting any louder. Shouldn't they be coming this way?

"Little pinch coming up," said a voice.

I opened my eyes. The inside of my parents' Honda looked different. More spacious. Much better lighting. And the ceiling was white.

I saw a face I didn't recognize. "Ouch!" I instinctively let out after feeling a sharp pain in my left arm.

"Sorry my friend- just an intravenous."

He looked at me and winked. The paramedic was a young man-maybe early thirties.

"You're gonna be just fine," he said. "By the way, the I.V.'s in."

I was lying completely flat on a board of some sort barely able to turn my head. I reached up with my right hand and felt a hard collar around my neck.

"That's a precaution. It's a c-spine collar- a cervical spine collar. You'll have it on up until the time the docs clear your neck of any fractures or injuries," he said.

A beeping sound was emanating from something near my feet.

"No, don't lift your head. I don't want you to hurt yourself," he said. "That's just the monitor making that noise. I undid your shirt so I could place those electrodes on you so I can observe your heart rhythm. All that wiring just leads to the screen. What's your name?"

"Ty."

"D'you know where you are, Ty?"

"Ambulance."

"And do you know what month it is?"

"March," I said. "How's my uncle? And my brother?"

"They were picked up by the other crew so I can't answer that right now. You're lucky you had your belt on. Your car's in pretty bad shape."

"How bad?"

"Bad. You owe your seat-belt." He hung my komboloi up in front of my face where I could see it. "Did you have this in your coat?"

"No."

"Well I found it lying on the middle of your chest inside your coat when I put the leads on." *On my chest?* "I'm gonna leave it here next to you and when we get to Brigham, I'll pass it over to the nurses so they don't lose it. What d' you call this thing anyway? Worry beads, right?"

The ambulance slowed down then came to a halt. Its sirens were replaced by the short, high-pitched sound of an oversized vehicle in reverse. The driver got out, came around, and opened the rear doors. The legs on the stretcher were extended, and the two paramedics wheeled me into the building, past a short hallway, and into a well-lit room where a large crowd was waiting.

"Let's move him over. One, two, three." The group transferred me with the backboard onto a hospital stretcher. I could barely shift my arms because two additional safety straps had been tightened across my lower chest. A bright light shone down from above compelling me to keep my eyes shut.

The paramedic called out: "Eighteen year old belted driver in three vehicle collision on the FDR. Significant damage to vehicle. Blood pressure: one thirty over eighty. Heart rate: nineties. He is alert and oriented times three but experienced positive loss of consciousness. Additional passengers being extricated as we speak."

"What's your name?" said a hoarse male voice.

"Ty," I said, as I felt each of my arms now being extended in either direction by faceless others.

"Do you know where you are, Ty?"

"I'm in the hospital."

"Did you black out, Ty?"

"I think so."

"You been drinking?"

"No."

"Open your mouth."

I opened it.

"Airway patent," he said to the group. "Now take a deep breath in."

I breathed in and out as the cool metal of a stethoscope probed my chest.

"One more- in and out," he said.

I felt a tightness around my left arm.

"Equal breath sounds," he called out. "Let's put him on the monitor and get me a pressure please."

"Don't worry honey. That's just the blood pressure cuff," a sweet voice whispered into my ear. "One twenty over palp," she added in a much louder tone.

"Ahhhh…" I felt a sudden sharp pain in my right forearm.

"Just another I.V., buddy," said a different male voice with an Indian accent.

"Let's go. Cut! Cut!" said the hoarse voice.

I felt a draft over my lower body as my slacks were shredded with what must have been gigantic scissors. The nurse placed slimy stickers on my fully exposed chest.

"Put him on the monitor please," a new, authoritarian male voice called out.

"Open your eyes," said the hoarse voice.

A flashlight was shone directly into each of my eyes causing me to blink.

"Pupils five millimeters, equal and reactive," said the hoarse voice.

I shut my eyes again to escape from the dazzling ceiling light. I felt tugging on my underwear and before I could react it was shredded and removed along with the rest of my clothes. I was lying there completely naked with a dozen strangers circling me.

"Little prick coming up," said the voice with the Indian accent. "Listen bud, we're still trying to get another I.V. in so bear with me and don't move your arm."

I tried to move my left arm to cover my privates, but it was also being tugged on. Sharp pain in my outstretched arms, stripped naked, bright light from above- I was being crucified!

"Can you cover me up?"

No response. More commotion. I felt a second razor-sharp pain in my right arm above the prior spot.

"He's got a five centimeter laceration in his left scalp. It's not bleeding," said the hoarse voice. "Listen, don't move your neck, OK? Don't move your neck. I'm gonna take the collar off just for a second so I can look behind it."

"OK," I said. With all the ruckus, the only way I could distinguish whether someone was speaking to me was by their leaning over and yelling into my ear.

He removed the front of the collar, and I could feel his fingers pressing on the back of my neck. "This hurt?"

"No," I said and instinctively shook my head.

"Don't move your neck! If you have a c-spine injury, you might end up a quad," he yelled. "How 'bout this? Does this hurt?"

"No."

"This? This? How 'bout this?" he said shifting his fingers up and down the center of the back of my neck.

"No," I said.

"C-spine non-tender," he called out to the group as he refastened the collar.

"Can you cover me up? I'm cold," I said.

"Finish the secondary," said the dominant male voice.

The hoarse voice was now pressing on my ribs. "Does this hurt?"

"No."

He pressed on my belly. "Does your abdomen hurt?"

"No."

I felt pressure on my pelvic bone on either side followed by someone squeezing my thighs and calves before raising each of my legs off the bed and bending them one at a time at the knee.

I began to shiver. "I'm cold."

"Yeah, well, it's rainy outside. It's still winter," said the hoarse voice.

"Alright, move on," said the doctor in charge. "Let's turn him. We're gonna go to his right. One hand on the shoulder, one hand on the pelvis," he said directing the team. "Listen, my friend. You just keep your arms across your chest and we'll do the rest."

I realized my hands had been released and covered my privates.

"One. You- I don't know your name- hold the c-spine. Two. Three."

My entire body was rotated onto my right side.

"This hurt? How 'bout this? And this?" said the hoarse voice. I answered 'no' in succession as he pressed firmly along the middle of my back.

"Lube," he said.

Someone was touching my behind. All of a sudden, I felt a horrifying sensation I never knew existed. I lost my breath and clenched my teeth. My eyes welled up.

"Good tone," said the hoarse voice.

"Listen, you have to tell him you're going to do that before you do it. This guy probably doesn't even need a rectal," said the voice which I was now certain was in charge.

"Can you cover me up?" I said.

"Get us a warm sheet, please," said the same voice. "And let's get our X-ray- just a chest. Lift the board up."

The backboard was hoisted off the bed, and a flat object placed behind it.

"X-ray!" called out a new voice- a woman's.

People started shuffling away. I looked to my left then to my right. No one. I lifted my head up off the backboard and realized I had been left alone with a female X-ray technician- a young blonde with full lips. I caught her staring at my penis.

"Take a deep breath in," she said.

BEEP.

"All clear," she yelled and with that everyone stormed back in.

"GET ME A FUCK'N SHEET NOW!"

I felt a warm, cotton sheet placed over my body. I raised my left arm and located an area on my scalp where I was suddenly aware of a stinging pain. I could feel a gash and dropped my hand down to where I could see it. My fingertips were stained red. I stared at the fresh blood then dragged my fingers through my hair and looked again. The blood was still there, but there were also small tufts of hair between my fingers. I repeated the motion. More hair. Mounds of hair.

A new female voice: "We got another one coming in from the same accident. This one's real- unresponsive and hypotensive, intubated in the field."

"Listen, scan this kid's head only," the dominant voice said. "We'll clear his neck clinically when he gets back. Don't scan his abdomen. He doesn't need anything else. If the scan's negative, sew up the laceration and move him along."

"I found his wallet- Timos Karos," said the sweet voice.

"Good. Will somebody please call his parents?"

****

A sterile towel was draped over my face, as the doctor- a young but confident resident- placed the last of nine stitches into my scalp. I heard my parents' whispers beyond the curtain.

"Everything alright?" my father asked in a flat tone which provided me no insight on the condition of Philip or Uncle Timos.

"Everything looks pretty good," the doctor said. "His head CT's negative, and I'm almost done with this then he can go."

"Thank God," my mother let out in Greek.

"A little topical antibiotic gel and voila, drape can come down, and you are all set," the doctor said uncovering my face.

"This'll match my uncle's scar," I said.

I sat up and wrapped my body in the bed sheet. My eyes were readjusting against my father's navy blazer when all light faded to black as my mother's torso swallowed me in a hug.

"Phil's outside in the waiting room. He's fine," my father said. "They just did an X-ray and said everything was normal."

"They're still working on Uncle Timos," my mother said without letting go. "They wouldn't let us see him."

"Is he hurt bad?" I asked.

"He's pretty banged up," the doctor said while disposing his instruments. "You're lucky. You got away with just a scratch considering- the perks of being young."

"I'm gonna need some clothes," I told the doctor before turning to my parents: "They tore them all up."

"That's just part of how we handle trauma patients," the doctor said. "It's hard to distinguish right away who's sick and who's not. Part of what we need to do is strip patients down quickly to determine what injuries they have. Don't worry. We'll give you some scrubs on your way out."

I dragged my fingers through my hair and pulled out some more strands. "My hair's falling out."

My mother glared at the doctor.

"It's the stress," my father said.

"That's what I think," said the doctor. "I've seen it once before. You must be very susceptible to stress. It should get better by tomorrow."

"I don't get stressed- not like this."

"We all get stressed. Maybe because you're not used to it, your body's responding a little differently," the doctor said. Turning to my father, he added, "Let me give you your son's discharge instructions."

The doctor walked out and my parents followed. A nurse came in and handed me a set of blue paper scrubs and a clear plastic bag which contained my torn-up clothes, my shoes, my wallet, and my komboloi. I stood up, drew the curtain shut, and put the scrubs on. The nurse then directed me to an empty waiting room in the emergency department. Figuring my parents had gone to find Philip and Uncle Timos, I sat down and waited.

I pulled the komboloi out and began fidgeting with it. I shut my eyes and leisurely rolled the beads one after the other along their string each time anticipating the subtle tap of stone against stone. I took slow deep breaths. The accident was upsetting enough, but everything that followed made me feel violated. Was process more important than patient? I could do it better. My heartbeat- where I sensed it in my neck- was slowing. I took another deep breath and pushed the next bead forward. It was working.

"Don't go," an exhausted male voice shouted from a patient care area outside the waiting room. "Don't go!"

I leaned over to get a better look. The voice had originated from behind a thick blue curtain.

"Don't go!"

I left my things and nonchalantly walked towards the curtain. The drapes suddenly retracted forcefully, and a white coat appeared from behind. The doctor- a bald, bearded man- drew the barrier closed once more not affording me the opportunity to see inside.

A nurse in pink scrubs walked up to the doctor. I was close enough to hear their whispers.

"She's taking her last breaths now," he said. "I wanted to get the husband in there before she went."

"Love you. I love you," the man wailed from behind the curtain.

I felt the back of my neck stiffen.

"We cleaned her up so he wouldn't see her with all the blood and vomit-," said the nurse, "doesn't make for a good final memory."

I tried to catch a glimpse through a small gap in the swaying curtains.

"I'm coming. I promise you. I'm coming," the man sobbed, his voice cracking and fading.

The doctor came over to me. "Can I help you?"

I felt my face get warm and didn't answer. He looked at my baggy paper scrubs and must have figured I was a volunteer.

"Fifty-three years of marriage," he said bobbing his head back and forth.

The nurse drew the curtain open to silence a beeping monitor. I looked over her shoulder at the ragged, wrinkled face of an elderly woman stretched out on a hospital gurney. Her thinning gray hair stood straight up. Her eyes were shut, and a long tube was sticking out of her nose. She seemed vacant but relieved. Her frail husband was leaning forward in his chair, his elbows buried in the mattress holding her purple hand up to his face.

"I'm coming," he said, his voice trailing off into a whisper.

The scene pressed up against me. It nudged me in. *Could this happen to me?* Surrounded and forced to acknowledge the possibility, I made a wish much like I used to before blowing out birthday candles: I hoped I would die first. The agony if it happened the other way would be a torment I didn't think I could withstand.

I hurried back to the waiting room. A door at the far end of the emergency department swung open, and my parents and Philip appeared. My brother was wearing his own clothes although they were dirty and disheveled. I looked at my father. He had a grim look on his face. I looked at my mother. Her eyes were red and swollen. I knew right away.

****

I paced around the emergency room cognizant of pins and needles radiating from my neck all the way down my back. I was in a trance. Was it possible? Was that it- his time had passed? I looked at my fingernails and was surprised to see how quickly they had become withered and jagged.

The doctors were 'preparing the body'- whatever that meant- for my parents to view. Although my mother was the greater obstacle, she reluctantly caved in to my demand to see Uncle Timos one last time.

The same doctor who had sutured me escorted us down a long empty corridor. At the last minute, Philip decided he didn't want to go and returned to the waiting area. We stopped at a heavy metal door near the end of the hallway. Before letting us through, the doctor casually explained how all the tubes and catheters had been removed from Uncle Timos' body. He then swiped his ID and pushed the door open. "I'll give you some privacy," he said and disappeared.

Uncle Timos lay flat and motionless on a stretcher. A spotless bleached sheet covered his body up to his chin. Only his head and his left arm were exposed. A piece of red gauze was taped to the right side of his forehead partially covering his old scar. There were scattered cuts and abrasions across his cheeks and nose. His raccoon eyes were swollen shut. His face was pale and colorless.

None of us spoke although my mother's sobbing displaced the silence.

"You OK?" my father asked me.

"Fine," I said.

I had answered truthfully. Uncle Timos appeared peaceful. But as I began to stare more intently at his face I sensed an emptiness.

I looked closer searching deeper into his person. I discovered an undeniable hollowness. This wasn't my great-uncle. He wasn't in the room at all. This was something else- an imposter. The body I was staring at no longer had anything to do with Uncle Timos. He had separated from it. He had merged with the void. This was clear as day and it terrified me.

****

His body was sent to Athens for burial two days later. My parents accompanied it, while Philip and I remained behind to complete our semesters. I learned that the church ceremony was standing room only. The anguish which my family felt and the uproar of grief from strangers were not surprising. My great-uncle had helped hundreds and many hundreds more loved and respected him.

I never cried- not once. Uncle Timos had loved me like a grandson, but throughout that distressing period, all I could do was intellectualize his death as that of a good man who had lived a beautiful life. Tears wouldn't come.

Chapter 10

It was on a Saturday morning in mid-April. I woke up close to noon which was much later than usual. Something didn't feel right. I had been out with some friends the night before, but I hadn't stayed up late or gone drinking. I got out of bed that morning and pulled up the horizontal blinds. It was a muggy, rainy day in the city. I called out for Philip and even looked inside his room but it was empty. I poked my head into my parents' bedroom knowing they wouldn't be back from Greece for another week.

I turned the TV on in the living room and surfed past every channel twice before turning it off. I went to the kitchen, opened the refrigerator door and pushed it closed without noticing what was inside. I opened it again before realizing I wasn't hungry. I walked into the bathroom and stared at my reflection in the mirror. I ran my fingers through my hair and looked for strands. There weren't any and hadn't been for a couple of weeks now.

Back in my room, I turned my box radio on. WPLJ was playing *Holding Back The Tears.* Or was it *Holding Back The Years*? I became aware of my own breathing. I turned the music off and started pacing round and round my bedroom. I looked out the window again, but there was no sign of blue.

I felt a sadness. I wasn't sure why. College would begin in the fall. I had settled on Trinity and would be moving to its campus at the end of August. Was I anxious about school? Maybe about leaving home and being on my own? This feeling was unfamiliar. I had no understanding of what this small tremor was.

Miranda and I had been finalizing the dates we would set aside to see each other this coming summer, and I was keyed up for it. She had plans to go to Santorini with her mother and uncle, and I suggested that this might be the ideal place for us to meet. Although I would be pressed for time with college orientation hovering, I had to see her. I sat on my bed and fantasized about our reunion. I imagined myself on the beach beside her, but that April morning even this was difficult.

I couldn't focus. I had to do something other than reflect. I needed to be active.

I went back to Philip's room where I found a pad of drawing paper and a sharpened pencil. I sketched a figure, first by outlining a face and torso then sequentially filling it in with more and more detail. A woman was taking form. I had her looking over to one side somewhat expressionless. I erased the mouth and penciled a new one in, but this only made her look angry. I tried fixing it by darkening the area around her eyes and brows but that didn't work either so I lengthened her hair in the front to cover her eyes. As her arms took shape, they were crossed adding to her disconsolate expression.

I wasn't a rookie. While Philip stayed up late to paint, I often used to doodle beside him. I wasn't nearly as good and what I drew was usually more concrete like a fighter plane or a sports car. This time, my mood was driving me rather than the usual boredom. A little bit of imbalance makes art better. Funnel that directly onto the paper or canvas or music staff. Inspiration through raw, inherent emotion- an advantage that's not available to the average artist.

Two hours passed. I finished the drawing and moved it to where I could admire it. I used it as a guide for my next poem.

Ma Femme Fatale

A toast to you, ma femme fatale,
May romance prosper for I love you.
I feel our bond, so strong, there can never be another.
You alone are mine.

Yet, I live a life unfulfilled,
For each night, I lie without my one,
My one true love, ma femme fatale.
For you have yet to live in me,
Our roads run parallel.
All I can do is sit quietly,
And love you sincerely,
And hope that one day soon we finally meet.

I felt better, rejuvenated. I read the poem again and then the telephone rang.

"Guess which one of your buddies is going to his first choice?" Rob said.

"Who?"

"I'm goin' to Stanford," he said. "I got the call last night. They pulled me off the wait list."

"Congrats."

"I am so psyched. My number one. I got my number one."

"That's great."

I was happy for my friend. Even so, as high school came to an end, I kept Rob in the dark about my summer plans with Miranda. Maybe he suspected I wasn't being completely honest with him. Maybe our personalities and interests had changed over senior year. Either way, Rob and I were no longer as close as we had been. It was mutual. I knew Rob would be successful in his life, and although I never heard anything from him or even about him ever again after high school ended, deep down I always wished him well.

I got on a gray suit with a white shirt and a striped tie. Mykonos in the middle of the afternoon. Warm out. No breeze. Beach is empty.

I have my bathing suit on. Walking into the water. Refreshing. Small fishing boats surrounded by some larger yachts further out. Swimming. Away from the shore.

Where did the yachts go? Where are the rest of the boats? They're all gone. I should get back to land. This way, I think. No, is it this way? No, this way.

Where did the beach go? It's covered with water. I'm alone. I'm alone in the middle of the sea.

Small ripples growing into white-capped waves. Current's strong. I'm getting tired. So tired. Not gonna last. But there's nowhere to swim to. I'm in the middle of the ocean. A vast ocean.

Exhausting! Water's getting in my nose. I can't struggle like this! I'm tired. Please. What can I do? Maybe lying perfectly still I can save some energy? Perfectly still. Won't move at all. I'll try and float here.

It's not working. The water's getting into my eyes, into my nose.

Help me. I gotta try louder. Help me. Please, help me.

Please. Please.

Wipe my tears.

I'm going under. I'm gonna drown.

Gasp.

Tum…Fshhhhhhhhhhhhhhhhh

I can't breathe. Gasp.

Tum…Fshhhhhhhhhhhhhhhhh

It's a dream. It's only a dream.

"Dr K. Relax now."

Tum…Fshhhhhhhhhhhhhhhhh

I can't die in my dream.

"We're giving you something. Just relax. You'll feel better in just a second."

Tum…Fshhhhhhhhhhhhhhhhh

I can't die in my dream.

Chapter 11

In the early afternoon on August first, the ferryboat I was travelling in docked on the island of Santorini. In the dry, one hundred degree heat, I boarded a bus to the main town of Fira. My T-shirt and underwear were soaked with sweat and the twenty-pound duffel bag I was lugging wasn't helping.

Thirty-five minutes later, I had arrived. Peering over the edge of the cliff down at the Aegean, I recalled the little I knew about this wonder- how the island's volcano collapsed on itself thousands of years ago with a crescent-shaped portion of the mountain's rim left standing while the rest imploded and submerged into the sea. Water molecules chaotically filled the *void*, and Fira was built on the rim of the old volcano where it endlessly surveys a center which is no longer real. All eyes look past it anyhow and simply admire the infinity beyond. I had stood on this narrow thoroughfare with the intense view years ago and remembered my name for it- sunset strip. Miranda and I had coordinated in some detail to meet at this very spot- the site with the unobstructed view of heaven- at seven o'clock this evening.

Embarrassed to ask my father for any more money than he had volunteered to give me, I couldn't afford a real hotel so I left the strip and began trudging along the town's stone-paved, inner roads looking for a cheap rental room. Although my parents knew I was meeting a friend, they had been good about not asking too many questions. They knew my answers wouldn't be satisfying anyway. It felt odd being abroad without them for a second consecutive year, but the time and place that Miranda and I had settled on was fixed. Since my father's work dictated he be in New York this month immediately after which they planned their move, the calendar conflict was irreconcilable.

I walked by a youth hostel advertising cheap rates in drachmae on a green chalkboard and decided to take a look inside. An apple-figured brunette wearing a U.S. military tank-top over floppy breasts stood alongside a greeting counter. Her flimsy shirt exposed the skin on her flanks, while a generous behind spilled over the sides of her tight jean shorts. She wore sandals on her muscular legs which featured ankle bracelets galore.

"American?" she said.

"Yes," I replied.

"I'm Jessica."

"Ty."

"Where from?"

"New York."

"Hey, I'm from Jersey. Are you staying the night?"

"I…maybe."

"Good," she said.

"And you're…"

"I'm spending the summer on the island, you know, working here, meeting new people, having some fun. You want me to show you 'round?"

The youth hostel had three sections- one for men, one for women, and the third for couples. Jessica walked me to the men's area, which was a single large room with ten or twelve bunk-beds three feet from one another resembling army barracks. I left my bag there and followed Jessica up two flights of stairs to a spacious outdoor roof garden or, as she referred to it, 'our family room.' As in Mykonos a year earlier, there were faces and complexions from all over and despite the severe heat the garden had a soothing balance which I found comforting. This would do. I paid Jessica a small deposit and headed to my bunk to get organized.

I quickly got over my initial excitement after I saw the restrooms which Jessica had neglected to showcase. There were two side-by-side stalls in a closet-sized room with a wet floor and no locks on the doors. Both toilet bowls were clogged with paper towels while three dozen flies hovered between stalls. Disgusted to touch anything, I flushed the first toilet with my foot, but it was beyond repair. The second toilet had a more primitive system that involved a corroded chain hanging from a ceiling unit. I yanked on it, and the entire, rusty metal module came loose and nearly fell on my head.

The male showers had a series of eight spouts none of which hung from a height greater than my own. I undressed and turned the knobs but had to bend down to get under the water, which had the pressure and flow of a stream of urine. The red knob was for show. While I was rinsing off, two men walked in wearing nothing but flip-flops. Maintaining male shower etiquette, we ignored each other and avoided any unnecessary eye contact. As I diluted the last remaining suds off my face, I heard Jessica's voice.

"Hey guys, we don't usually provide towels," she said, "but here are a couple in case you haven't had a chance to unpack."

Jessica was standing by the door with her back to us dangling three white towels over her shoulders.

"Merci," said one of the two foreigners grabbing one. I had brought my beach towel into the showers but took one anyway and secured it around my waist.

"I wasn't expecting such great service," I said.

"I try," she said still with her back to me. "Covered?"

"Yes."

Jessica stepped onto the wet shower floor as the nude Frenchman made his way past her drying his hair with the towel she had given him. The other naked guy went on showering as if he were alone in the comfort of his own home. He even started humming.

"I bet you get hit on all the time in this place," I said.

"Sometimes." Jessica leaned back against the wall and tried to push her hands into the potential space of her jean pockets before giving up.

"Do you ever shower with the guys?"

"Women are allowed everywhere around here," she said with a sinister smile. "No exceptions."

"I'm just kidding."

"Although there hasn't been a single guy yet who's told me the showers are off limits. I think most of you get a kick out of it, you know, showering with a girl around."

"I'm fine with it," I said.

I sucked some air in when I noticed Jessica looking at my chest. She quickly worked her way down to my legs before glancing back up to the middle of my towel. She locked eyes with me again. I reflexively looked at my watch without reading the time.

"Well, enjoy your stay, Ty, and definitely let me know if I can do anything for you."

****

I arrived at the strip a few minutes early and perched myself up on the ledge. The sea was a long way down. I wondered if anyone had tried to end it all, maybe a jilted lover angling for a romantic way to prove himself.

A young woman- probably my age and definitely Greek- was admiring the view just a few feet away. Wearing a short scarlet dress with white stripes, she looked like she belonged in a Chanel ad. For a second, I thought it was Miranda, and my heart bounced on a wasted adrenaline surge. I watched as four men approached her. Even before hearing them speak, I could tell they were Italians. They proved it by nonchalantly walking up to Chanel girl and starting up a conversation. No prior discussion between the men. No premeditation. No thinking through all the angles. They did what came natural. One of them was holding a stack of plastic cups and a bottle of red wine. Within minutes, the five of them were socializing along the ledge intoxicating themselves slowly. I was envious. Italians know how to enjoy life. This comes naturally to them. Greeks are a close second, but Italians are the masters.

A young gypsy girl who was barely four feet tall and carrying a white painter's bucket full of long stem red roses patted me on the knee.

"For your wife," she said in Greek.

"I'm not married," I replied also in Greek.

She gave me a pitiable look.

"OK. Ένα μόνο," I gestured with my index finger to be clear before reaching for my wallet. She handed me a single rose as I gave in to being fleeced.

I saw the Italians gesturing to one another as a girl in a white dress walked briskly past them. Miranda smiled, and my hand migrated over my heart. My Italian friends looked over and I winked back to prove to them I also understood what matters.

"Hi, beautiful."

"Hi, Ty!"

Miranda was taller than I remembered and was wearing a gold pendant with three interlocking circles. She was glowing.

"I missed you," I said.

We kissed on each cheek, and I hugged her.

"And where did you get that beautiful necklace?" I said.

"Oh, some strange guy gave it to me," she said. "But you never told me what it meant... that it's religious... the three forms of God. At least that's what somebody told me."

"I had no idea," I said. "You haven't been here before, right? To Santorini?" Although I asked, her letters had told me she hadn't.

"Never," she said. Her eyes widened as she looked behind me. "It's beautiful."

"The sun's gonna set soon, and it's reeeee-eally nice from this spot."

We stepped back and sat on the ledge.

"I'm sorry I'm late," she said, "but the boat trip took longer than we thought. Wow! It's a long way down."

"Who else came with you? Your mother? Not just the two of you?"

"And my uncle. My mom's at the hotel resting. I mean we just got here like ten minutes ago. We came with my uncle's boat." Miranda stretched her neck out. "There it is," she said pointing to a large blue and white yacht parked on a small pier at the bottom of the cliff.

"Pretty boat."

"It's a great boat," she said. "Ty, I'm so happy to be here."

From the opposite end of the concourse, we heard the escalating sound of violins. Three musicians supporting their bowed instruments on their shoulders headed a small procession. Wearing a light gray suit and a white dress-shirt with the top button undone, the groom followed closely behind flanked by two dozen men presumably close friends and family.

"I love weddings!" Miranda sprang up with excitement in her voice. "Let's follow them. Oh, and by the way, is there something that might be for me?"

Miranda looked me straight in the eyes as I handed her the rose. With a slight downward tilt of her head, she maintained her stare as the velvety red petals caressed the bottom of her nose and upper lip.

"What?" I said.

"You're blushing," she replied with a smile. "C'mon. Let's go."

I looked over at the Italians. Three had their eyes on Miranda, while the fourth had cornered the girl in the red dress. One of them motioned at me with his chin and raised his cup. In broken English, he started singing and his buddies quickly joined in: *"...at long last love has arrived...and I thank God I'm alive...you're just too good to be true...I can't take my eyes off of you..."*

****

We followed the procession to a tiny white church with blue shutters just around the corner from the strip. Escorted by her father, a

Barbie bride arrived a few minutes later, and the soon-to-be husband and wife entered the church arm in arm followed closely by the handful of guests who were able to squeeze in behind them. Miranda and I peered in through a half-open window on the side of the church opposite the cliff.

"I'm not sure this necklace will go with my wedding gown. I might have to take it off," Miranda whispered.

"Oh, I don't know about that. I think it goes with everything."

"Ty, I lo-o-o-o-ove your letters. Don't ever stop sending them to me."

"Same," I said with the most sincere tone I could evoke. "Where're you staying?"

"Our hotel isn't far from here. It's got the same great view like before. What about you?"

"At a youth hostel," I replied.

"A youth hostel?" she repeated. "Why?"

"I don't mind," I said. "It's an interesting group of people from everywhere."

"And where do you say you're from? Do you consider yourself Greek or American?"

"When I'm in Greece, I can't say I'm completely Greek 'cause I'm not- I've lived in the States all my life and my English is much better. But what's strange is that if I'm in the States and someone asks me where I'm from, I say I'm Greek."

"So in Greece, you feel American, but in America, you feel Greek. I can relate, although maybe I feel a bit more Italian."

We looked back inside the church. All eyes rested on a black-robed, gray-bearded priest with a rapper's crucifix around his neck. The uncharismatic clergyman waved his arms around with unconvincing holiness, while plastered toothy smiles prevented the majority non-believers from laughing out loud.

"This island is the best place in the world to be with a girl," I said. "Mykonos is fun, but it's better to go there with the guys or in your case with girlfriends. This island is more about getting to know someone, and, you know, getting inside them."

"Is that right, Ty?" Miranda said with an amused smile.

"I...you know what I mean."

Sweat lined every forehead in attendance. I wiped some off my own. Fortunately this was the short version of what is often a ninety minute ceremony. We watched as the magical man of the cloth guided the couple in a circular orbit around the altar. The temporary lack of oversight was exploited by the guests as the delicate silence dissolved and the crowd turned festive.

"Tell me more about your year- things you didn't write in the letters," Miranda said. "By the way, congratulations on Trinity. Excited?"

"I guess," I said.

"I'm so proud of you. I knew you were so smart from the first minute," she said. Miranda stroked each of my cheeks with the bloom of the rose. My eyelids drifted closed. When she pulled the flower away, I opened my eyes and realized that the early evening's yellow had gradually evolved into a bright orange.

"We have to go," I said.

****

The sunset was at its peak as we walked back onto the strip. Those crazy Italians were playing opera from a small cassette player. From where it rested on the pavement, I could barely make out the soft music, so I motioned to one of them who raised the volume between drags on his cigarette. His chum meanwhile had made progress now violating with gropes and kisses the innocence of my Chanel girl.

Miranda and I sat on the ledge facing the water thousands of feet below us surrounded by the panorama of a burning sky and a deep blue sea. Leaning our shoulders against one another, we looked out at the colors of life. Miranda reached for my hand and slid it over to her lap. At that precise moment, I was the happiest, luckiest person on the entire planet.

Chapter 12

Four sets of twenty-five push-ups had winded me but my motivation was strong. Miranda's uncle, who was staying on his yacht, planned to take the family and some friends for a swim at the 'red beach' on the back side of the island. Miranda had asked me to join them, and I hoped some vigorous early morning exercise in the roof garden might beef up my arms and pecs.

I found Miranda sitting alone on the front steps of her hotel drinking a frappe through a straw. She was enjoying the iced coffee Greek-style- lazily savoring each sip- so I sat beside her until she got down to the froth. After bargaining the fee briefly with a local, we rode a couple of donkeys along a narrow wind down to the port below. Miranda's donkey rode ahead of mine and throughout the twenty minute descent I was mesmerized by her slender frame as she bounced up and down the animal's back.

The yacht was massive up close. We boarded by way of a thin wooden plank with a steel railing and for the first time I was introduced to the mother whose name was Maria. She was leaning back in her chair with her veiny legs up on the boat's outer banister leafing through Vogue. In her late fifties, she was a bony woman with puffy lips and darkly tanned skin dripping in oil. Her two-piece exposed decades of blotchy sun-damage and merely highlighted her perfectly round implants even to my untrained eye.

After a short but uncomfortable burst of prerequisite small talk, she got down to business.

"So what do you plan to major in at school?" she asked me with a smoker's voice in her strong Greek accent.

"I'm not sure, maybe medicine, but I guess that's not a major."

"That's so much work. Do you want to do that to yourself?" she asked while turning the page. "There must be doctors in your family."

"My grand-mother's brother."

"I have much respect for doctors," she said unconvincingly. "And your father? What does your father do?"

"He's a diplomat," I replied feeling she already knew.

"Greeks love their politics," she said rubbing an ad and sniffing her fingers. "Do you have any interest in political life?"

"Not really," I said.

"And what about shipping- our traditional profession? Do you have interest in pursuing shipping- like my brother?"

"No, I don't think it's for me. I mean it makes for a good living, but, well, I just don't think it's for me." I knew nothing about shipping beyond FedEx.

"Maria, leave the kids alone. They don't want to talk to you," her brother interjected with a broad smile and a calm nothing-can-ever-break-my-stride voice. He was an older man, also thin but muscular, with thick black hair and an even fuller black beard. Maria said little else to me over the course of the afternoon, although I caught her looking in my direction more than once usually while blowing smoke over her shoulder.

Miranda showed me around the yacht which had a crew of eight working for the uncle. The exterior was all-white except for a deep blue, angled plexiglass windshield. In the rear, there was a comfy outdoor area with a rooted wooden table and pod stools, while the yacht's interior contained a spacious modern living room and kitchen, five bedrooms including a large master suite, and five baths all spread over the two lower levels.

In standard fashion for a Cycladic August, it was desert hot with a royal blue sky. Miranda and I stripped down to our bathing suits and climbed to the front of the boat where we reclined against the enormous blue window. Miranda's undersized fluorescent orange bikini exposed much of her small breasts and made them appear larger. She wore bright red lipstick and Jackie O sunglasses which swallowed up her tiny face. Unlike her mother, her skin was a pale white while her upper back was riddled with little brown moles. All twenty of her nails were colored a softer shade of orange. Around her neck hung my gold pendant which intermittently blinded me with the sun's reflection.

When we were far enough away from the port, the yacht's mighty engines were roused and the vessel began to power its way around the island. A sea breeze kicked up and kept us cool. Meanwhile, classical music could be heard playing from anywhere on the yacht. Two dozen speakers had been strategically planted both inside and outside to combat wind gusts. When we reached open sea, someone changed the music to the soundtrack from *Phantom of the Opera*. I recognized the overture immediately having watched the musical with my parents on Broadway during its opening week earlier in the year. As the Phantom's voice bellowing with passion and anger burst through the stereo system, his raw emotion contaminated my own mindset so much that I wanted to jump up and swing my arms around like a conductor. Thankfully, I restrained myself.

Miranda opened her beach bag and removed a lipstick and lotion. She shut her eyes while applying another layer of 'ruby red' then squirted some creamy goo into her palm and smeared it on her arms and shoulders.

"Do you want me…?"

"Maybe later when I flip over," she said anticipating my offer. She pulled out a pack of Marlboro and a lighter from her bag.

"Do you smoke in front of your mother?"

"My mom's sitting in the back. She won't get up," Miranda lit the cigarette and exhaled a puff. "Will you smoke it with me?"

I knew she was watching as I took the butt from her and examined it with a slow twirl between my thumb and index finger.

"Ty, are you a virgin?"

I froze.

"You know- a cigarette virgin," she said.

"No, I've tried them but I just don't get it. It really does nothing for me."

I noticed the moisture and lipstick residue on the end of it so I stuck it in my mouth marijuana-style and pursed my lips around it. I only inhaled a trace of smoke before handing it back.

"I don't think there's anything wrong with waiting for the right person," Miranda said. "I definitely think it's the right thing to do."

"Are you?" I asked.

"What d' you think?" she said. The sun burned through the dark lens of her sunglasses and I could see her big eyes staring back at me.

"I'm not sure," I said.

"I'll tell you if you tell me," she said.

"That's not an even trade. I'm a guy, and I'm older."

"So?"

"It's different."

"Why? Because you're not expected to be? Because you're a guy and your eighteen? That's dumb. I would actually like it more if you were." Miranda looked away, inhaled, and blew it out. "So you definitely wanna be a doctor, huh? You know Kelly's decided to go pre-med."

"Really? She didn't strike me as the type," I said. "I think I want to, but I'm not a hundred percent positive."

"Well, if you do, I want you to be a heart surgeon."

"Why a heart surgeon?"

"Well, don't they fix broken hearts? What's worse than a broken heart?" Miranda giggled.

"A shattered skull?" I joked although she didn't appear to find it funny.

"You're not afraid of sharks are you?" she said.

"Should I be?"

"Just so you know, we're not gonna swim on the beach. We're gonna swim in the deeper water around the boat," she said.

"Great," I said leaning over to get a sense of how far down the bottom was.

"What *are* you afraid of, Ty? Are you afraid of anything? Anything at all?"

"When I was younger, I was afraid of sleeping. I think I was afraid I wouldn't wake up- that I would *never* wake up," I said. "Sometimes I used to ask my mother to stay in my room until I was asleep because the process of getting to sleep made me uncomfortable. When she was in my room, I felt a bit more at ease letting myself fall asleep. I don't know- maybe I'm not as tough as I look?"

"You don't look very tough, Ty," she said.

"Thanks a lot."

"That's it?"

"Let's see. I think I'm afraid of dying?"

Miranda put her hand up to her forehead like a visor: "Dying?"

"I honestly believe this is our one and only life," I said. "I don't think there's anything else after this. That's why we really need to make sure we absolutely enjoy every minute of this one and that's why I wish you didn't smoke."

"Ty."

"The whole premise of a heaven just doesn't make sense to me," I said.

"Ty!"

"Live in the moment," I said.

"TY!" she yelled before looking away.

"What?"

"Stop!" Somehow I had hurt her, and she was pleading: "Stop it!"

I remembered that her father had died. The next song off the soundtrack wasn't as upbeat. The mania I had been feeling earlier was gone.

****

The volcanic lava which followed the massive eruption had given rise to sand and pebbles which maintained a burgundy stain all these centuries later. We arrived in the waters off the red beach at noon, and the crew positioned the boat about two hundred yards offshore. The heavy anchor had an endless length of chain as it plummeted down to the sea floor.

Miranda and I were leaning on the starboard railing staring at the hilly terrain's red hue. Her amiable cross-examination was ongoing.

"If you had to choose," she said, "what you want most- power, fame, money- which one would you choose?"

A question I couldn't possibly get right. "I'm not interested in fame," I said. "Money's OK, but I don't think I need that much of it to make me happy. You know Freud said that only fulfilling our childhood fantasies really makes us happy and since making money isn't a childhood fantasy, it can't truly buy happiness."

"Ty, you didn't answer the question."

"I think I would choose power, followed by money, and then fame."

"Why power?"

"Well, those things I told you I'm afraid of, money and fame can't help me get over them but maybe power can."

"How?"

"Well I don't mean power over people- more along the lines of an internal strength."

Miranda grinned.

"What?" I said. "How would you answer it?"

She shrugged. I stared at her until she looked the other way.

"Miranda, are you bored of me yet?" I said.

"Don't worry. Honestly, don't worry. I'll let you know when I'm bored of you," she laughed.

"Thanks."

"Are you bored of me yet?" she said losing the smile.

I had prepared for it. "Ask me again when I'm ninety-five and lying on my deathbed and my life is flashing before my eyes and my answer will be exactly the same: Not just yet."

Many of the guests- all considerably older and none of whom I cared to meet- had already gone into the water. Some dove in, while others descended more gradually by way of a four rung ladder in the back of the yacht. Miranda grabbed my hand: "Come with me!" We went inside through the kitchen, where the crew was preparing cold cuts and a traditional Greek salad. Miranda led me up some steps to the third level then onto a narrow spiral stairway up to the highest point on the yacht. Lifting each leg one at a time over the railing, she positioned herself onto a small ledge with her back to me clutching the rail with a firm grip.

"Follow me down," she said. "You'll follow me down, right?"

I nodded.

"Leap of faith, Ty."

"Not a huge fan of leaping," I said.

"Don't let me down." She took a deep breath in and jumped. Headfirst! This wasn't her first time.

"I promise," I mumbled to myself.

Miranda was underwater for what seemed like a long time. When she finally resurfaced, she dried her eyes and looked up at me.

"C'mon."

It was a long way down, but I had no choice. I maneuvered my legs over the railing. I counted to three under my breath and sucked in as much air as my lungs could hold. I repeated this drill a second and then a third time before jumping- feet first. As I penetrated the surface, a gush of salt water rushed in through my nose. The cold water temperature made me realize how overheated my core had gotten sitting in the sun all morning. I dog-paddled towards the light surprised at how deep my body had submerged. I finally helped myself to some oxygen and wiped my eyelids with wet fingers.

The water was clean and clear but looking down from the surface I couldn't make out the bottom.

"My uncle says it's about a hundred meters down," Miranda said swimming over to me.

The stereo was still on and with the engines idling we could hear the music. I recognized the next track- *All I Ask of You*.

"This song," I said still trying to catch my breath. "I love this song."

I didn't think Miranda heard me, and then I saw water splash into her eyes and she became completely distracted or so I thought. "We'll make this our song, Ty. This'll be the song we dance to," she said affectionately pushing the side of my head with her palm before swimming with a gentle breaststroke out into open water.

Chapter 13

A dozen round metal tables were scattered around the youth hostel's roof garden, while thin steel arches enveloped by flourishing grapevines protected guests from the seething rays of the sun. Miranda dropped by the following morning to surprise me. To avoid her seeing my 'room' or the repulsive lavatories, I had quickly whisked her up to the garden. There we wrote postcards to friends in the States and listened to *The Joshua Tree* while splitting the earpieces on my walkman. Our connection had progressed as silence between us was now comfortable.

Jessica was there serving coffee, orange juice and muffins. She glanced over a couple of times, but I avoided eye contact. After the breakfast crowd had thinned, Jessica aired out a beach towel in a sun-drenched area outside the archway's shadow and settled onto it plucking her T-shirt off in the process. She took her time rubbing Coppertone on her already tanned breasts then patiently swatted at them to ensure a single square millimeter hadn't been neglected. I pretended not to notice, but Miranda tapped me with her pen and directed my gaze with her eyes.

"Very comfortable with her body," she whispered putting on her sunglasses so as not to be caught looking.

I stole a dizzying glance at their lustrous shine and felt an urgency to change the subject. "Where are you going after this?"

"We're going to Turkey with my uncle."

"Oh, wonderful," I said. "I guess I won't see you for another year." Immediately after it came out, I wondered why.

Miranda lowered her head shifting her eyes over the upper rim of her sunglasses. Our eyes met and she held steady for a second or two before looking back down at her postcards. She didn't say a word.

****

That evening, Miranda went out to dinner with her mother and uncle. I picked up two take-out souvlakis with pita and 'the works'- certainly a tasty alternative to any fancy restaurant. Sitting on the white-washed stairs of a random home near the heart of Fira, I inhaled the juicy grub while watching waves of tourists strut by.

With only a handful of fashionable walkways in Greek island towns, I wasn't surprised to see Jessica strolling by. Alone, wearing black bell-bottom jeans, red boots, and her military tank top, she pulled up as soon as she saw me.

"I saw you on the roof this morning," she said. "It's great up there, right? Relaxing. It doesn't just whet your appetite for life, it quenches it."

I chewed, smiled and nodded all at the same time.

"Are you having a good time with your lady friend?" she said crossing her arms and swaying her torso from side to side. "She's very pretty."

Jessica was on a fishing trip. I continued nodding without getting up.

"She is," I said before stuffing the last morsel of tzatziki-drenched pita bread into my mouth.

"Listen, I've been meaning to ask you," she said swaying more dramatically, "maybe we can keep in touch when we get back to the States." With both hands, she casually pulled her hair back into a ponytail and in so doing arched her chest forward hoping to sway my response.

"Sure. I mean I'll be in Connecticut for most of the time, but I'll be coming into the city on some weekends. It's only two hours by car," I said, "and since you're in northern Jersey, we can meet up in the middle."

"Or maybe I can come up to you- if I'm not imposing- and you can show me around campus."

"Sure," I said sipping my Pepsi through a straw.

"Will you remember to give me your number before you leave? Or you know what, let me just get it from you so we don't forget," she said.

I pursed my lips to try and hide what I was thinking- how is it that spending time with an attractive woman peaks the curiosity of other women who in turn make that extra effort to try to identify what exactly that unique special thing might be? Or maybe she just thought I was a nice guy.

Jessica pulled out a blue Bic from her weightless cloth purse. From the corner of my eye, I saw Miranda approaching. The situation was unsalvageable.

"Hey, you're done already," I said to Miranda as I stood up.

Jessica politely introduced herself, while Miranda's smile longed for sincerity.

"So what is it?" Jessica said.

Miranda watched me recite my Manhattan phone-number to Jessica who scribbled it on her palm. Each digit was more agonizing than the one prior.

"Super," Jessica said. "Well, enjoy yourselves." Jessica grinned at Miranda, who was looking the other way then smiled broadly at me before walking off.

"She's from New Jersey," I said. "She asked me for my number back home. I felt bad."

"She's like a prostitute," Miranda mumbled.

"She waits on tables and works the check-in…"

"Ty, who cares?"

"Oh. It's just…"

"Let's go for a swim."

"Now? Where?"

"My hotel."

"The pool's not closed at night?"

****

There was no sign of the moon. I certainly looked for his distinctive mark hoping for guidance. Although I briefly thought about passing by the youth hostel to pick up my bathing suit, I reconsidered when the dual images of a shitty toilet and an uninhibited Jessica flashed through my mind. I wore boxers under my jeans and figured these would do.

So as not to wake her mother, Miranda bypassed the front entrance and delicately snuck into her hotel room through the ground floor veranda's sliding-glass door which they kept unlocked. She came out bathing suit in hand.

"Why didn't you change?" I whispered.

"She's a light sleeper."

Miranda led me through a narrow dirt path to the pool which was dimly lit by underwater lights. The water was tranquil and crystal-clear.

"This way," she said. I followed her to a grassy area behind two giant bushes. "We can change here."

"Where?"

"Spin," she said.

I turned around and felt her hand pushing on my shoulder as she steadied herself to remove her jeans. I closed my eyes and held my breath.

"You can look now."

Miranda was in the same two-piece she wore on the boat.

"Go ahead," she said. "Now you change."

"I'm gonna wear my boxers," I reminded her.

"Fine. Then I can watch."

I removed my canvas sneakers, my Lacoste shirt, and finally my jeans, carefully adjusting my boxers to minimize tenting.

Miranda covered her mouth and snickered.

"What?" I asked.

"Nothing."

We laid our clothes by the side of the pool and tested the water-cold but tolerable. Briskly but without splashing, Miranda pushed her way in to about waist level and dove in. She came up and free-styled across the pool before supporting herself on the far ledge.

"Get in," she whispered loudly.

I walked into the water pausing a few seconds after each step. By the time I was in, Miranda had drifted back.

"Ty, look up. Look how nice the stars are. I want you to think of me every time you look up at the stars."

No problem.

Miranda swam around me. She wrapped her arms across my neck and straddled me with her legs. I felt her breasts pressing up against my back as every muscle in her body suddenly pitched in for a reverse bear-hug. I remained motionless as she let her feet drift back down to the pool floor. She then dropped her arms around my abdomen resting her head along the middle of my upper back. Under the privacy of water, she pressed her index finger deep into my bellybutton twirling her fingertip to get further in.

"Yours doesn't go very far," she said.

"It's a useless accessory."

With her index finger still in the hole, I could feel her stroking my lower belly with her other fingers. My days in an all-boy school began to haunt me. Was this all a big tease? Was she too young? Was

I sure she'd kiss back? Would I not be a gentleman? I was too far behind to figure things out on short notice. I gently took hold of her arm and turned to face her.

"I'm not going to kiss you," I said.

Her eyebrows narrowed. "Why did you say that?"

"Because I thought about it- about kissing you."

My whole body was pulsating. I moved in closer and placed my hands on her waist. I could feel the goose pimples on her wet skin. Her slick, glossy hair and shiny eyes sparkled. I wanted to- more than anything else in my life. Only our heads and shoulders were above water. My heart was pounding so hard I thought she might hear it. Miranda stared at me with the same stern look. Unexpectedly, there it was- the sign I needed. Subtle but noticeable: I could *hear* her breathing! Shallow and rapid and through her mouth. She was panting, waiting for me. Patiently waiting for me.

It was perfect. Simply perfect. Too perfect.

"GET OUT OF THE POOL." A hotel employee ran out onto the deck and started yelling in Greek. "GET OUT OF THE POOL! NOW!"

Miranda and I quickly floundered out of the water, but the guy kept shouting. He even began cursing at us. I ran and grabbed our clothes. When I spun around to find Miranda, her mother was parked directly in front of me in her bathrobe.

I hoped for a phrase. I would have settled for a word. But instead, only an anemic, incomprehensible yelp leaked out of my mouth. I looked pathetic standing there all wet and dripping in my filmy boxers, which by now provided a neatly sculpted silhouette which candidly portrayed my sentiments for her minor daughter.

"Miranda, do you know what time it is? It's time to come home."

Chapter 14

Miranda must have put up quite a fight. Somehow she convinced her mother to allow her to spend that final night with me. I knew this would be our 'farewell dinner' but did my best to stay upbeat. I kept a smile on as she approached our slated meeting point at the rusty gate outside Skala- a popular taverna known for its traditional island delicacies.

She was wearing a boy's white long-sleeve dress shirt over a black mini. Her legs were feminine but fit with the perfect bulge of muscle in her calves.

"You look fantastic," I said, "as usual."

Miranda thanked me more properly than I would have liked.

The staff seated us on the terrace directly along the edge of the cliff as I had requested. An enduring brick oven served as the taverna's centerpiece while candlelit blood-red tablecloths floated in a semi-circle around it. Already past dusk, the sea below us was black with flickers of concentrated artificial light where yachts and cruise ships were docked.

From the get-go, Miranda seemed pensive as I was doing the talking and getting mostly fragmented answers from her. After the waitress took our orders, I gave in.

"You're very quiet tonight," I said. "Not sure I like it," I added to lighten my assessment.

Miranda raised her water glass up to her mouth- "Tell me why," I said- and she brought it back down without drinking.

"After your last couple of letters, I was worried about you," she said.

"Why?"

"You talked about your uncle, and I know you felt bad about what happened and you said how you were sort of out of it and hadn't been sleeping real well."

"Yeah."

"And you said how you really wanted to meet up this summer to get your mind off things," she said.

I nodded.

"Well I was worried about you."

"What did you think I would do?" I said.

"I didn't think you would *do* anything," Miranda said. "It's just that how could I not see you after a letter like that?"

My head jerked back in disgust. "What are you saying- that I put pressure on you or something?"

"Not pressure," she said. "It's just that I felt...I felt..."

"What? Sorry for me?" I said. Miranda looked down at the table. "Is that what you're saying? You felt sorry for me? Please don't tell me you only agreed to meet me because you felt sorry for me."

"No, that's not why!"

"What is it then? What's bothering you tonight?

"It's not easy," she said. "It's not that easy! Is it that easy for you?"

"What?"

"Well, I'm not gonna see you for another year probably and I don't even know if we're comin' to Greece next year. And you're starting college. I'm sure you're gonna meet a lot of new people, and I still have three more years of high school, and I don't wanna be alone all the time. All my friends have boyfriends, and I wanna have someone, and I'm feeling all this pressure from everybody." She took a deep breath in and blew it out.

I said nothing giving her the opening to move ahead.

"I know you understand. I think you feel the same way," she said. "You know we can't go anywhere with this." Miranda stared down at her lap and waited while the waitress refilled our glasses. "And what are you gonna do? I mean, you'll be in college. Don't tell me you don't plan to date anybody- like that girl from yesterday. You're gonna see her. Are you just gonna talk about me the whole time?"

"Miranda," I leaned in against the side of the table and took hold of her hand. "I really, really like you."

Her eyes got red. I saw a tear begin to inch away and gently tightened my grip. I moved in closer to kiss her, but she pulled her hand from me and turned away.

"What're you doing? Are you listening to me?" she said. "Did you hear a word I just said?"

I covered my face with both hands embarrassed for a few seconds before feeling plain anger. I hated drama more than anything. Part of me knew she was right. Somehow, I had been repressing the difficult truth that we wouldn't be able to sustain anything.

"Ty, I like you too, you know that, but if we were meant to be together…" *Please don't say it, Miranda. Please don't say it.* "…it'll just happen."

Those predictable words spilled out and suddenly she appeared fake. What a cheesy line! What a phony thing to say! What a child she was! I was fuming inside but did my best not to show it. The stars and the smallest crescent of moon were out over the water. I focused on them feeling flustered and ashamed.

The food arrived just as the conversation grinded to a halt. We scattered our tasteless entrees around our plates while that next half hour passed painfully slow. Without considering dessert, Miranda argued we go Dutch on the bill. I insisted on paying, and after we got up she thanked me with an obligatory peck on the cheek.

We walked back to her hotel in silence. When we got there, she unexpectedly took hold of my hand.

"I'm gonna miss you very much," she said.

"Have a nice time in Turkey," I said, "and don't eat any pork."

"Will you write to me? Please write to me."

"We'll see," I offered.

"No!" she released my hand. "Not 'we'll see.' Are you gonna write to me or not?"

"I'll write you."

She nodded. "Have a safe trip back," she said, "and remember the stars. We'll always have the stars, Ty, and the Greek islands, and *Phantom.*"

****

At dawn, I boarded the ferryboat to Athens alone. Over the Aegean, the wind was wild and the boat swayed forcefully. The up and down and up and down made me nauseated sitting inside so I stepped out into the elements and found a seat on a deserted wooden bench along the side of the boat. With my eyes shut and my sweatshirt zipped up to my chin, I welcomed the full impact of the blustery gusts across my face knowing I couldn't cope with this amount of turbulence on the inside.

Miranda was in my head every single second of that eight hour trip. All the minuscule details from the last three days had to be replayed and reviewed again and again. I derived a toxic pleasure reviving our time together- burning every smile, every glance, every odor, every soft embrace into permanent memory. But the frustrating manner in which things had broken apart at the end dragged me down. More than any other time, I felt like I had been placed in a trance- staring endlessly nowhere at nothing. Halfway to Athens, I felt the urge to get it out. As I put it down on paper, I periodically gazed up at the horizon longing for her.

Let Love Be

Don't think so much
That's been my advice to many
It's not good for you
Like that cigarette
Thoughts come like the flame
But what slowly burns is not paper

Only one heart
One queen down yet more to come
The rest is numbered and black
Fold
Lose something now
You can only gain it back later

I believe in my words
So why don't I follow them
I overanalyze
I sit to think about something
Staring endlessly nowhere at nothing
The crown missing from my head
I cannot reign happily

No ace of spades in your back pocket
Play to win
But look away from that mirror
Behind your opponent
Or else you'll win a meaningless game

So here I sulk
Wishing my life away

Too many emotions
Don't think about them
Don't bother
You'll never understand each and every one

So why can't I do it
Why can't I... not think about anything
Or at least think about something unrelated
I try desperately
To channel out my mixed emotions
To put my feelings into words
To possibly understand why I feel the way I do
This is why I write poems
To end the hurt that thinking back brings
To stop looking at nothingness
And seeing only what is not there
To hopefully understand
Forgive me
To hopefully reexamine
This love that I have for you

I left for New York two days later. On the flight back, I felt better although I didn't have a whole lot to look forward to. The stress of moving to a new place and dealing with college life would soon be upon me. My parents were moving to Europe probably for good. I had already been deprived of the wisdom and support of my great-uncle, and now somehow I had lost the affection and friendship of my little Miranda.

The atmosphere around me had transformed. Everything appeared different. Everything was different. The changes petrified me.

The day after I arrived in Manhattan, I mailed Miranda the poem without a formal letter. I decided this would be the last poem I would ever send her. Miranda must have understood how difficult a time it was for me because I never received anything in return.

Chapter 15

I opened my eyes and glanced at my alarm clock. It read 3:05 A.M. in green neon. I rolled onto my side and tried to go back to sleep. I turned the other way but couldn't get comfortable. Finally, I sat up suddenly wide-awake. This wasn't jetlag. I had been back in New York for five days and had more or less acclimated.

I felt strange- anxious, nervous about something. I turned on the light, kicked my sheets off, and wandered around my bedroom then out into the living room. My parents weren't in town, but I knew Philip was asleep in his room so I kept the apartment lights off. In the dark, I walked around our glass dining room table three or four times- tapping all eight black lacquer chairs each time around- before returning to my room. I sat down on the side of the bed and took a couple of deep breaths. I reached for some magazines and leafed through a few pages of *People* and *SI* but found myself staring beyond the photographs. I was looking but not seeing. I couldn't focus. I got back up and resumed my pacing around the shadowy apartment. *What's wrong with me?*

I went back to my bedroom and turned on the TV. I didn't have cable and most of the stations had static or infomercials at that hour. I stared at the screen for a few minutes before getting restless and shutting it off. I went to the kitchen, flipped on the light switch, and opened the refrigerator door. I wasn't hungry and mindlessly repeated the sequence in reverse. I jumped into bed again and lied down. Before I could get comfortable, I bolted upright and whispered out loud: "What's wrong with me?" Clenching my teeth, I repeated it louder and with anger in my voice: "WHAT'S WRONG WITH ME?" This wasn't about not being able to sleep. I felt an uneasiness, a restlessness, that was dramatically foreign. Something wasn't right.

I got back up and spread the horizontal blinds. The pavement outside was wet, and I could see windblown rain in the light of the streetlamp. The sidewalks were barren and lonely. Was I sick?

I walked to the bathroom and stared into the mirror. I stuck out my tongue. I looked deep into my own eyes. I spread open my eyelids with my fingers searching for a clue. I felt all along my neck- nothing obvious. I felt the urge to go and peed what seemed to be a larger volume than usual. "Maybe I have diabetes?" I whispered to myself. Was that possible at my age? I felt a sudden discomfort on my left side. Was this the side of my spleen?

I walked back to my room and plopped down on my bed. I closed my eyes and tried to relax but instead I felt like I had to get up and run. I desperately wanted to strike a punching bag as hard as I could. I clenched my fists tightly until my face was burning and my hands were shaking and then I began to cry. Discreetly but hard. It was so rare an occurrence that it felt not only odd but wrong. Was this me? Was it the fact that I hadn't cried in so long? Had everything merely built up?

I sobbed for the next few minutes trying to push it all out. Finally I dried my face and waited another few minutes to allow any evidence of the event to fade. I turned on the hallway lights and started pacing around the apartment again making a little more noise than before. It worked.

"What's going on?" Philip said in a groggy voice as he walked out of his bedroom.

"Can't sleep."

"Jet lag?" he said walking towards the bathroom.

"I don't feel great. I'm not sure if it's…"

Philip interrupted me with a machine gun fart.

"Chinese food last night," he said before shutting the bathroom door.

Why did I think Philip could be helpful?

Whatever this was, I was going to get through it on my own. That's the way I've gone about things, and it's always worked for me. But I needed something to get me through tonight- this one night- since I knew I'd be better with the dawn. I shut my bedroom door. It was difficult focusing at first, and I did get up more than once for no real reason, but going over it again in my mind helped me through those early morning hours and that's all I had hoped for.

Alone in the Dark

By God, a bad dream. Another sleepless night alone.
There is no noise to be heard as the house is empty and safe,
But the fear inside and in his mind, it creates the noises.

It wants to come out, to exhibit itself, to make its presence known.

"Bad boy. Go to bed." These words echo within his mind,
But what is the use. In bed, he will never find nor feel rest.
Yes mother knows best, but that which she asks is not that easy,
So he hates the evening and the night for a good sleep he cannot find.

The fear that he emits cools his face and body.
Oh, this boy's tale is a very sad story to tell I fear,
For all this danger that he so much dreads is nonexistent.
And no person can correct how this boy feels. There lies the tragedy.

You see this boy's fear is not around him in his home.
It lives within him and inside him as it feeds on his needs.
Sleep is something that he just must find on his own without help.
And herein rests the problem- he must meet the unexpected alone.

He feels that when dreams arrive, he will travel somewhere.
All alone, his spirit will fly as his mind feels only sleep,
But wherever it goes, will both mind and body stay healthy?
And what if he never wakes and stays trapped in a place where no one cares.

Everybody needs to believe in something higher.
Where there is unhappiness, religion appears as does trust.
When there is difficulty, believe there exists Another,
Someone who will always watch over you when fear sets your mind on fire.

I reread the final verse wondering whether I believed it. The reassurance which faith in a kind and gentle God provided was soothing, but the greater part of me found it difficult to accept. An all-powerful God who is all-loving *should* be able to wipe out despair and provide us with a good life *without* compromising free will. There may well be a God, but maybe His focus isn't any longer on us. It's probably our own selfishness and self-centeredness as human beings which compel us to believe that His spotlight must constantly be turned our way.

Had I stumbled onto something? All of a sudden, I saw a legitimate solution to the problem of evil. Our omnipotent, loving God may exist; He's simply turned his attention elsewhere. Like a proud parent letting go of a child who's grown up, He's allowing us to explore His world and make mistakes and shape our own futures. But He Himself has moved on. I shook my head back and forth in disgust.

Alone in the Dark was not to be shown. It bore too much of my own internal struggles. It reinforced my doubts. What I didn't know at the time was that it would be the last poem I would write for a decade. What I also didn't know was that the next four months would be the nightmare of my existence.

Chapter 16

My parents had replaced our old Honda with a new Honda and despite the accident trusted me enough to grant me unrestricted use. I drove up to Trinity's campus on the final Wednesday of August one day before orientation. Unfortunately no one was available to help me get settled. Mom and dad were swamped with last minute chores before the move, while Philip who had voluntarily signed up for summer courses was in the middle of finals week. My former classmates were scattered around the country for their own orientations, and Rob I hadn't seen since we shook hands on the front steps of St. James Church on the Upper East Side after graduation.

I dragged two large suitcases into a three-story Gothic dormitory building called Galen Hall and checked in at the student housing office. Apparently I had been allocated a single room- instead of the standard double- in the freshman lottery, a draw which I had no recollection of having signed up for. At the time, I was skeptical whether this was actually good news since I was actually looking forward to having a roommate.

Except for a small tan desk with a wooden chair, a single worn mattress on its rusty metal frame, and some basic kitchen appliances, the second-floor space where I would be spending the next nine months was empty. I did have my own bathroom which was a big plus. I closed the door, dropped my bags and instantly dashed to the window. The view was simple, ordinary- green oak trees in the foreground swaying from a gentle, late summer breeze with a vast central lawn behind. I looked behind me at my new home and sighed. I really was hoping for some company.

****

During a chaotic and disorganized orientation, I signed up for Biology I, Intro to Philosophy, Calculus I, and Computer Science I- a challenging schedule but one which I certainly could handle. I planned to keep with the school's liberal arts curriculum emphasizing the biological sciences with a pre-med timeline in play- just in case.

Once classes began, Philosophy unexpectedly turned out to be my favorite. I was fascinated by the ancient Greek philosophers and spent as much time reading about them and their ideas as I did Biology even though Bio was much more labor-intensive. Unlike my high school philosophy course, I immersed myself in the readings almost as if I had something at stake. Epicurus was the man- so misunderstood. As I read more about him, I found his religion to be less about orgies and debauchery and more so a logical road map to inner peace. I spent hours upon hours in my room studying him and his teachings even pulling books from the library which were outside the assigned reading list. The common sense which he employed to simplify a complicated world was undoubtedly well ahead of its time. I immersed myself in his logic while looking out over that endless lawn and felt a familiarity, even a soothing comfort, mixed in with his ideas.

Although Mr. Tsai was nowhere to be found- he had probably graduated- I did recognize Cybill in philosophy class. Always dressed in black from head to toe, her scrawny frame consistently waltzed in ten or fifteen minutes after the bell. I hoped she didn't remember me and made no effort to become re-acquainted. Surprisingly, during a number of philosophical debates during the first couple of weeks, Cybill and I expressed similar points of view. In a handful of instances, we even argued in unison defending a shared opinion in a team-like fashion only to be confronted and sometimes condemned by the professor and some of the other more vocal students. Fortunately with nearly one hundred people in the class, it was large enough that I never had to establish eye-contact with her. Cybill and I backed one another without formally acknowledging each other and that was fine by me. I never liked that witch.

****

The first month of college passed smoothly, uneventfully. By early October however, the calm began to blow away. On successive nights, I had difficulty falling asleep. This had nothing to do with my soft as a board mattress or the fact that there weren't any ambulance sirens and car horns to make me feel at home. It started with a peculiar sensation. As soon as I got into bed and shut my eyes, I felt my eyeballs gyrating rapidly under my eyelids. It took an hour- sometimes two- before I finally dozed off, and the next day I would wake up with a dramatic fatigue which a poor night's sleep couldn't justify. Getting up in the morning became a struggle, and I was late to 9 A.M. Biology- not a good thing given the cutthroat pre-meds in the class.

During daytime hours, something also felt off. I was lethargic- practically every minute- even when I did get a full eight hours of rest. The symptoms were subtle and invisible. When I spoke to classmates or stayed occupied with activities, I would forget about the sluggishness for a few minutes, but as soon as I had a moment to myself- especially if I was alone- it quickly resurfaced. Something wasn't right.

By the middle of the month, I was having more problems concentrating. This would usually get worse as the day went on. Homework began to take me twice as long, and I couldn't complete assignments without getting up and pacing around my dorm room every so often to quench a nervous energy. The final outcome of my efforts ended up a lesser quality than I had been accustomed to. Falling behind on bulky reading assignments and watching as my grades began to drift only produced more stress. A vicious cycle was settling in.

With the daylight hours growing shorter and shorter, my mood followed the sun god down. Feelings of pure sadness set in by evening and I felt increasingly abandoned. Students were bonding, going out, having fun. I didn't have the energy or the interest to do any of it, so I retreated to my room after class aware that I was becoming more and more isolated. Around the same time, my appetite went away. Some days, I wouldn't eat anything until dinnertime, and even then I had to make a conscious effort to put something in my stomach. When the scale at the gym showed that I had lost six pounds, I ran out and bought two bagels at a nearby deli forcing them down to try and reverse the imbalance.

I was alone in my dorm the afternoon of Halloween. Although there were parties starting all over campus, I wasn't planning on leaving my room. The unexplained sadness within me had yet to peak but was sufficient to distort my sense of true reality. I *had* to be physically sick, I reasoned. There must be something desperately wrong. This haunting feeling terrified me so much that I put on some sweats and jogged to Trinity's library. There, I plucked out a medical text with a section on signs and symptoms of common diseases. Within a half-hour, I had made the diagnosis: adult-onset diabetes mellitus. This is what I had suspected back in August, and now my symptoms had simply gotten worse. I was still peeing more than usual, and this was specific evidence for the condition. It was frustrating knowing I could never step back into my untainted identity.

I went straight from the library to a CVS outside campus where a pharmacist helped me pick out a urinary sugar detection system. Back in my own bathroom, I peed on the strip and stared at it for the next fifteen minutes. It appeared negative, but I couldn't say for sure. Should I repeat it? Was this diabetes at all? The exhaustion, the lack of energy- these could be signs of a much more sinister condition maybe even something life-threatening.

Staring into the bathroom mirror, I frantically pressed all over my body with my fingers. I moved from one site to another poking and prodding deep and hard. I checked my armpits, my neck, my groin. I left one area red and sore before moving quickly on to the next. Finally, there it was. I felt a small knob on the right side of my head which threw me into a panic. I paced around the room twice before darting to the phone to call Philip.

Although I spoke with my brother every three days or so, I hadn't told him about any of this. I honestly believed I would eventually figure things out. But tonight- on this pagan night of goblins and ghosts- I needed to hear a familiar voice. I longed for some support.

After some small talk with Philip, I nonchalantly tossed it into the conversation.

"I wish you could feel this," I said.

"What is it?" Philip said.

"I have this bump on my head I've never felt before."

"So what?"

"Do you think it might be something bad?"

"Like what?"

"I don't know- like a brain tumor?"

"Brain tumor?" There was silence on the other end. "Yeah, that's probably what it is." Philip waited another second or two before reverting to a quasi-concerned brother. "You schmuck. A brain tumor's in your brain not on your scalp. If it was a brain tumor, it would be on the other side of that thick skull of yours." In his own blunt way, Philip provided me with some mild albeit transient reassurance. "So last week, you thought you had breathing problems- remember how you were short of breath? Then you thought you had diabetes."

"I might have…"

"Now you think you have a brain tumor. Ty, snap out of it! There's nothing wrong with you! You're just stressed out about college."

I sighed blowing into the phone. I desperately wanted to 'snap out of it' but it wasn't as simple as that.

"I don't know," I said. "I can't concentrate. I get these headaches. And I'm tired all the time. Something's wrong."

"There's nothing wrong with you! You're fine," Philip said.

"I know I *look* fine- that's one of my problems. That's why nobody sees it. So tell me why am I so stressed?"

"You wanna know what might help?"

"What?"

"You really wanna know?"

"Yes."

"Have you tried your right hand?"

"Maybe I should see a doctor."

"Fine, maybe you should. Maybe if you hear it from a doctor, you'll feel better. You obviously don't believe me."

****

My private room- deemed a lottery victory by most freshmen- was impinging on my psyche. Whenever I took a break from pacing, I'd sit with the lights off staring out the window at the rain and cold which steadily descended on New England. The formerly broad-leaved oak trees were by now exposed and vulnerable, while the landscape beyond was growing increasingly gloomy and bleak. My reflection was constantly there on the glass despite my best efforts to look past it.

I didn't schedule a doctor's visit since a part of me was afraid of what he might find. But when I came across yet another concerning physical finding, I convinced myself that an expert opinion was mandatory and proceeded to the college's health services.

"It says here you have a mass in your scrotum," a cocky young doctor wearing a filthy white coat read from his nurse's note. He appeared skeptical.

"I think so. It hurts down there and I know men get testicular cancer at a younger age."

"Younger than who- women?" the doctor said.

I didn't laugh and so after examining my privates he punished me with my second rectal exam of the year. It seemed every time I came across a doctor, I got a finger in my ass. I buckled my belt and gently placed my rear down on the chair to hear his assessment.

"I don't see anything wrong," he said scrubbing his hands in the sink. "The boys are happy. That bump you feel is your epididymis." *My what?*

I left his office dissatisfied and returned to health services the following morning. I had to wait outside for an hour and a half since the office didn't open until eight. I saw a different doctor this time who fortunately had some gray hair. His history-taking was much more thorough as he asked me to elaborate on each of my symptoms making a note of every one- my poor appetite, my fatigue, my difficulty concentrating.

"Tell me more about the low energy," he said in a voice which sounded like Reagan's.

"I'm not sure if it's real fatigue," I said. "I feel a certain tiredness all the time, but it's like a nerve fatigue rather than a muscle fatigue. If you asked me to play basketball, I probably could. Does that make sense?"

He took his time with the physical exam as well and waited until we were both seated before offering his opinion.

"Well, first of all, I don't feel anything in your scrotum. It feels normal. Second, just looking at you, you're very thin and you're at an age where developing diabetes is uncommon. We can check a urinary glucose, but I expect it to be fine. What I do want to know leads me to something else. Any time I have a patient with a whole lot of unrelated complaints, I sense a different kind of problem." He hesitated. "Is there anything specifically that's bothering you or worrying you? For example, are you stressed at school?"

"Sure I am."

"How about your home situation? What's going on at home?"

"No problems there. My parents have always been very supportive, and we get along great, but they did move to Europe a few weeks back."

"So what kind of support groups do you have here? Are there any other relatives nearby? A girlfriend maybe?"

"My brother's in New York," I said. "No girlfriend."

"Well, I'll tell you what I think," he said removing his thick lens glasses and rubbing his eyes until they were moist and red. "All these events in your life- a new school with new professors, much more difficult courses, moving to a new place out here, add to that the loss of the family support structure now that your parents are abroad- these are all very powerful stressors. There may also be others that are not as apparent to you that may need to be brought out. The symptoms you're feeling may be the result of all these stressors coming at you at the same time. I think you might have depression."

Depression? Up until that day, I thought 'depression' simply meant extreme sadness. Could it affect so many aspects of my life? Could depression make me feel this sick?

The doctor elaborated and presented a good argument for his diagnosis. It made sense, and I even felt better just listening to him. Unfortunately, as soon as I walked out of his office, I began having doubts. I worried that he may have missed something. Why hadn't he done a more thorough physical- the last doctor gave me a rectal? Didn't my condition warrant an X-ray or some other test to be *absolutely* sure I didn't have something bad? And instead of asking me to come back in a week to see how I was doing, he scheduled me a new appointment with a psychiatrist! Not only would I have to tell my entire story to yet another doctor from the beginning again, but did it have to be a psychiatrist? *How embarrassing!* I'm eighteen, and I need to see a psychiatrist! I was disappointed in myself. I wasn't as strong as I thought. Not crying all those years- something I believed meant I was solid and thick-skinned- may have actually been detrimental.

Chapter 17

I skipped my scheduled appointment with the psychiatrist thinking I could manage but once again I was wrong. My sadness and my anxiety were feeding off each other and merely intensifying. The fatigue had become unbearable, and I was now having daily headaches on top of everything else. I stumbled in and out of classes like a zombie. Mirrors served as reminders of my new blank stare. Some students surely must have thought I was abusing.

In the middle of the afternoon four days after my last doctor's visit, I found myself alone in my dorm room curled up in a ball and crying worried I had a tumor that the doctors weren't able to diagnose. I gave in and called health services who told me to come right in to chat with the psychiatrist.

The shrink- a middle-aged woman in a blue pantsuit and sneakers- let me get through my entire story including my newest symptom without interruption.

"It's strange," I said, "but when I'm just about to fall asleep, I see a lot of flashing colors. Vivid colors. I've never had this before."

Right off the bat, she agreed with the last doctor's assessment except that she added the word 'major' to characterize the depression. She suggested that because the various 'neurotransmitters' were out of whack, what I was seeing was a result of the 'chaos' in my brain. She had much more to say, but I zoned out frustrated by how quickly I had gone from being a happy, in-love eighteen year-old kid to a pathetic tangled brain-wreck.

We talked about reality for half the allotted time and spent the rest of the hour analyzing my dreams. She seemed especially interested in this.

"So, for example," she explained, "if someone dreams of a bed with clean white sheets, this implies that his subconscious mind believes his worries are coming to an end. Do you remember any recent dreams you've had so we can discuss them?"

"I've had a few that have to do with school," I said. "In one, the teacher starts passing around exams, but I have no idea we have a test that day."

I agreed with her that this was school-related stress and didn't feel enlightened by her feedback. But when I brought up some more obscure dreams that made no sense at all, she started to delve deeper into each one and the cockamamie analyses she came up with almost made me laugh out loud even in my wretched state.

"I think the fact that you see yourself in the role of a jet fighter pilot shooting at enemy planes can mean many things," she said. "You wanna climb high in your life. You're ambitious and dream a lot. You strive to excel. Maybe you take risks. You're willing to fight for what you believe in. These are all good qualities I want you to know. But tell me, what are your feelings about this dream?"

I didn't have the heart to tell her *Top Gun* was on TV the night before.

She never prescribed any meds, and I saw her only one other time. I did take her advice on a few things. I dropped calculus which reduced my workload. I avoided all alcohol. And, I tried as best as I could to stay occupied- this was actually her most helpful recommendation.

Throughout this blue period, I avoided *Phantom*. I had no choice. The music stirred up emotions I couldn't handle. My depression not only distracted me from daily living, but it also prevented me from reaching out to Miranda. There were many instances when I honestly believed I was deathly ill, feelings that could crush even a young man's libido.

****

I jotted down little reminders on Post-it notes on how I could go about being less anxious. They were short, fortune-cookie-like pearls. I placed them in my book bag, stuck them on the refrigerator, or dropped them on my dorm room floor. Some I read and reread daily. Others I stumbled upon unintentionally. I hoped these blurbs of wisdom could direct me to the path towards the happy person I once was.

Philip took the train up to Hartford for the day on the grounds that he hadn't seen me in a while, although I suspected there was more to it. It sounded as if he wanted to scope things out. Either that or my parents had put him up to it. Since I hadn't exactly been reaching out to anyone over the last few weeks, I figured something like this was coming.

My brother walked into my dorm room and was immediately distracted by my collection of miniature yellow billboards.

"What's all this?" he said referring to the Post-it notes peppered across the wall above my bed. "'Life's too short. Just be happy,'" he read out loud having chosen one at random. "No shit?"

"Believe it or not, it's something we forget about," I said standing almost directly behind him. "You know how it is when you get all wrapped up in the daily routine."

Philip scanned to the next one over and read it slowly enunciating each word distinctly: "'Going into medicine will help me be less afraid.' What does that mean? Afraid of what?"

I sat down on the bed.

"Afraid of what?" he repeated.

"Dying," I said.

"Dying? You're eighteen! What's your problem?"

"Everybody's a little afraid," I said. "I just think that with medicine, I'll get to learn more about 'life and death' stuff, and maybe I can get more comfortable with some things that make me nervous. I mean if I can explain the things around me a bit better, I might be less afraid."

Philip had already moved on: "'It's not about 'dollar sign'. Maybe it's not about power either.'" He looked at me and shook his head. "Explain, genius."

"I'm starting to think these things aren't that important."

"Explain."

"What's the point?" I said. "How much can you have? How much money's enough? How much power's enough? I mean you always want more, right? What's the limit? When are you actually gonna be happy? Probably *never* because there is no limit. You're always gonna want more, so it's better not to crave for something hopeless."

"If you don't think money's important in this life, you're living in la-la land," Philip said. "It's gotta be the thin air out here in Connecticut."

"You're not gonna make any money, you idiot. Have you heard of the starving artist?"

"That doesn't mean I don't understand money's important," Philip looked back at my notes shaking his head. "Ty, you're losing it."

"Let's go out," I said. "Lemme show you…"

"What the hell is this? 'God is not as loving as we think.' Jesus, why are you wasting your time up here in college when you already know it all? You can't be sure of any of this shit."

"And are you absolutely positive that none of this can be known for sure?"

"Yeah," Philip replied cautiously.

"Then you just contradicted yourself."

"Ty, what the hell are you talking about?"

"Nothing. Don't worry. I'm getting better."

****

Despite more unwarranted optimism, the nadir did arrive. One afternoon after class, I was lying on my bed in and out of consciousness and intermittently dreaming. Suddenly I found myself wide-awake staring up at the ceiling, but I couldn't move. I wasn't able to twitch a single muscle. I panicked when without warning my great-uncle appeared. His dead body drifted towards me hovering over my bed. His eyelids suddenly parted, and he stared down at me through the polished yellow beads that had replaced his eyes. I couldn't react. This had to be a dream. But how? I was awake! I was paralyzed for what felt like a full minute although it was probably only a couple of seconds.

I burst out of bed. The hallucination was gone, but it had resourcefully left something behind: guilt. Devastating guilt. For the accident. For missing the funeral. For a premature death. Uncle Timos was gone forever. He hadn't 'passed on.' He had been erased. There was no afterlife. Death meant the end of the mind, and it's only the mind that matters. The body, the particles, the debris become irrelevant. When the mind goes, what use are the residuals? The individuality has been lost. Just as there was an infinite period of time before my great-uncle was born and developed into the person I loved, there would be an infinite period of time without him to follow.

Would Uncle Timos care about any of this now- now that he's gone? He isn't feeling any pain. He isn't feeling anything. He no longer exists. His death should be of no concern to me were it not for one unmovable fact- I desperately missed him.

****

I rushed back to health services and arrived five minutes before the staff had locked up for the evening. The nurses knew my name by now and sent me through to meet with yet another doctor. Direct and to the point, this pill-pusher was in a hurry to get out and not in the least bit interested for an extended chat. He glazed over my story and medical records as a formality.

"I want to start you on something just to take the edge off," he said scribbling chicken-scratch on his pad. "This is an anti-depressant-not one of the popular ones you've heard of but just as effective and safe."

"If you think I need it," I said.

"You don't have any other medical problems?"

"No."

"No history of liver disease, hepatitis?" he said. "Hepatitis is an inflammation of the liver. You've never had that?"

"No."

"You drink?"

"No."

"The main side effects of this drug are on the liver so stay away from alcohol."

"That's not a problem."

Along with the prescription, he handed me a sample of three tablets from a cabinet. He put on his coat and walked out of his own office ahead of me. At the first water fountain, I popped one into my mouth and washed it down. Perhaps the placebo effect came into play but an hour later I felt more relaxed.

Chapter 18

A ringing sound startled me.

"Hello," I said placing the phone up to my ear. It was either going to be my parents or Philip.

"Guess who," said a woman's voice.

"I don't know."

I sensed my heartbeat quicken.

"Take a guess!"

"Miranda?"

There was a pause.

"It's Jessica… from Santorini."

"Hey! How are you?" I said trying to recover by sounding extra-animated. "Where are you?"

"I'm home in Mahwah, in New Jersey."

"You've been good?"

"I have, and I dug up your number and then your brother gave me this one and I thought I'd call and see how you're doin'," she said. "How've you been?"

"Well- since you ask- I've been a little out of it lately, stressed out with school and things."

"Ty! Stress isn't good. It'll take years off your life," she said. "We have to find a way to de-stress you."

"No, I mean, things're getting better. I went through a bad stretch, but I'm OK. I'm getting used to the slower pace of life in Connecticut."

"Well, I know stress sucks. I work as a P.T.- a physical therapist- and I know my patients who are stressed out about things don't do as well. It really screws up their immune system."

I realized only then that I had never asked Jessica what she did for a living during the more rigorous seasons.

"Do you work every day?"

"As a P.T.? Yeah. The hospital's a few blocks from my place. I walk to work. It's satisfying, you know, working with patients, getting them stronger."

The conversation was soon flowing effortlessly. It felt good catching up with someone who rekindled memories of a pleasurable period. Jessica's baseline giddy personality made our chat even more fun.

"What's your sign, Ty?"

"Jess, I hate that stuff," I said. "Astrology's such crap. I'm not at all superstitious. I'm the enemy of superstition."

"C'mon. Play along."

"Fine. Pisces."

Jessica mumbled the horoscope reading to herself.

"Very interesting," she said waiting for me to bite.

"OK, what?" I said.

"It says here a beautiful woman will re-enter your life."

"No, it doesn't. You're kidding, right?"

"Yeah, I am. But it does say: 'Romance is looking pretty hot for you this weekend. With a shift in Saturn's moon to the north working in your favor, make sure to stay cool, casual and relaxed. Play your cards right and you may end up on top.'"

"It doesn't say that," I said.

"Actually, it does!"

"Read yours."

"I just did. You're not the only fish around here," she said. "You know what they say about us Pisces. We're supposed to be shy and timid and romantic people."

"Are you shy, Jess?"

"No."

"Are you timid?"

"No."

"Are you romantic?"

"I can be," she said. "I can be very romantic under the right circumstances and if I'm with the right person. I bet that's true for you too."

"Probably," I said.

"So when's a good time? Next week's Thanksgiving, but I can come this Saturday."

"Jess, we can always meet half-way if it's easier for you."

"No way. I've seen enough of the city, and I've never been up there."

"You're not missing much. But if you drive up, why don't you at least stay the night? I don't have a big room, but I don't mind crashing on the floor and giving you the bed."

"I'm honored. You mean come next Monday I can say I slept in Ty's bed."

****

Jessica would be arriving by early evening, so I spent the afternoon cleaning my filthy dorm room and discarding quite a bit of junk in the process. Rain drops were tapping on the window providing a fitting score to the tedious task at hand. When I was nearly finished I realized my pills weren't in the drawer where I usually kept them. I had been taking the meds for four days now and felt considerably better.

Since the hospital's health services were closed on Saturdays, it was vital that I locate my own batch. I searched behind the desk and under my bed. No luck. I felt under my bed sheets then rummaged through every desk drawer. I looked through the medicine cabinet in the bathroom and even got down on my hands and knees to check behind the toilet. Still no luck. I went down the hall to the dorm's disposal room and retrieved the white trash bag I had earlier discarded. Then I sat on the floor in the middle of my room muddling through the waste.

No sign of the pills. I suddenly felt deflated. I felt...powerless. I got up and started pacing. This was an absolute disaster! I looked out the window at the gray. Things just couldn't get any worse.

"Where the fuck is it?" I said, the muscles tightening in the back of my neck.

I was terrified. I dropped down on the floor and churned out thirty-five push-ups in rapid succession. I would have kept going if I had the stamina but my arms gave way. I bounced back up hyperventilating.

"Where... the fuck... is it?" I said louder.

I started pacing around the room again this time trying to catch my breath. The doctor had told me the medication wasn't addictive, so this couldn't be a withdrawal reaction. But there was no question in my mind that these pills were helping and that's why I had to find them. They would calm me down. I wanted to feel normal again. So utterly frustrating! I had finally found a remedy which helped me and I couldn't hold onto it.

My breathing felt labored. This was unbearable. I was slowly drowning. I ran to the window, pulled it open as far as it would go, and stuck my head out. I sucked in the humid air- five or six deep breaths- while heavy rain continued to fall. The November breeze against my saturated hair chilled my insides and I started to shiver. Resting my body on the windowsill, I turned around and faced the storm. The drops fell on my face like cool darts but I welcomed it. It was soothing. My tears were soon mixing in with the rain.

"Fuck you," I whispered in surrender.

My head was pounding. I slid down to the floor suddenly feeling severely nauseated. I desperately hoped I wouldn't throw up. There's nothing in the world that I hated more than vomiting. It hurt. It was painful to my core. Ever since I was a kid, I did everything I could to avoid it.

"Help me. Please, please, please help me. I can't take this anymore."

My own words sounded hollow. No one was going to help me. By now, there was nothing I was more certain about.

"Wake up, Ty. Wake up!" I said. "No one's gonna bail you out!"

I wanted to escape all this in any way I could.

"WAKE UP!"

It was going to be up to me and up to me alone.

****

I took down all the Post-it notes except for the most important- the one I knew from the very beginning contained the difficult truth about life and death. Human denial is strong, but I must be stronger. I left that particular message hanging from the refrigerator door and didn't care if Jessica saw it. I actually hoped she would.

The crying had helped, and I felt better especially now that I had a plan. I would call health services first thing Monday morning for a new prescription. I could make it through the next 36 hours since I had Jessica. Her timing couldn't have been more perfect.

I showered and put on some clean clothes. I brushed my teeth and was reminded by my reflection in the bathroom mirror that on the surface everything seemed fine. Yes I looked a few pounds lighter but otherwise normal. Total disarray on the inside, relatively sound on the outside. The devil- my internal crisis of faith- was hiding.

****

Jessica wore a brown bomber jacket over a white turtleneck sweater, a long skirt which ran all the way down to her ankles, and pointy cowboy boots. A lightweight gym bag hung over her shoulder.

"Well, well, stranger," she said. "How d'you do?"

"I do well," I smiled. "Come on in."

Jessica dropped her bag on the floor, removed her jacket and hung it on the back of the chair. She stretched her arms up from her shoulders extending her hands and fingers towards the ceiling. She sucked in a deep breath and drew in her abdomen. As she slowly exhaled, it was obvious to me she wasn't wearing a bra.

"Yoga?" I said.

She opened her eyes and smiled.

"Love it," she replied.

"Have a seat," I said.

Jessica had two options. She chose the bed.

"No posters. No paintings. No pictures," she said. "Ty, I think you need an interior decorator."

"I hate this room," I said. "I never cared to fix it up."

"The weather's awful."

"Did you find it easy getting here?"

"No problem. Some traffic around the city, but not too bad."

Despite a little more in the way of nerves now that we were face to face, Jessica and I kept the conversation rolling along. We started by sitting upright at either end of the bed. Fifteen minutes later, we were leaning back on our elbows with legs crossed facing each other. By the half-hour mark, we each had a pillow behind our head and the gap between us had dramatically shrunk.

Jessica was helping herself to a glass of water, when she paused to read my note on the refrigerator.

"Ty, what's this all about?"

"My little reminder?" I said.

"What does it mean?"

"Exactly what it says."

Jessica stared at it expressionless. "'Death is annihilation,'" she read out loud. "Did you write this on account of having a bad day?" she laughed.

"A philosophical day," I said. "But I believe it. There's nothing after this."

"That's sort of dismal to think about."

"That's why there's this thing called religion, otherwise we'd *all* be going nuts."

"So why on the refrigerator?"

"Just a reminder," I said.

"You'd hate to forget?" she smiled and sipped from her glass. "'Death is annihilation,'" she repeated looking back at the note. "I guess it's possible." Jessica walked back and sat in the tiny space which had previously existed between us. "What d'you suggest? I mean the clock's ticking, right?"

With her torso flat against the bed, she rested her head on the pillow and pulled her skirt up above her knees.

"Cool boots," I said.

Jessica crossed her legs aiming the toe in my direction.

"Should I be afraid?" she said staring at me from the corner of her eye.

"Once we die, it doesn't matter. There's no pain or anything. If we have to be something, I guess it's sad... that we're gonna lose each other's company."

"Well then maybe we should do some binge-drinking tonight and drown our sorrows," she laughed.

Although I was composed, I could feel my demons percolating. I was constantly keeping them at bay. Alcohol was a definite no-no. More importantly, losing touch with reality was *not* the point. It should never be the point.

"Why don't we just catch a movie?" I said.

"OK, but only if you hold my hand- especially after all this talk about death and destruction."

Although she certainly had no idea, Jessica's company and the distraction it provided for me were vital in that moment. The contour of her cotton turtleneck presented me with a different kind of distraction, but this I'm sure she was well aware of.

"You know, Jess, even though I don't know you all that well, I trust you with stuff that I wouldn't tell just anybody. I want you to know I like you and consider you a close friend, even though I don't know everything about you. So... what d' you say about that?"

Jessica awkwardly leaned in and planted a dry gentle peck directly on my lips.

Chapter 19

Jessica and I arrived back at the campus after watching an unbearable movie about the lightness of being. It was after midnight. The earlier rain had transitioned to a powdery snow. I parked the car in the student lot adjacent to the dorms and turned off the engine.

"Listen to the silence," I said.

We both stared at the snow which was falling in large sticky clumps and quickly accumulating on the windshield.

"So what happened to that girl you were hanging out with from the summer?" Jessica asked.

"Miranda?"

"Was that her name?"

"We sorta fell out of touch after I started college," I said.

"So you're not seeing her any more?"

"No."

"Was she your girlfriend?"

"Let's just say we had a connection."

"Friends who, you know..."

"Not that kind of connection," I said. "She's a close friend."

"I'm really surprised," she said. "You guys never fooled around? You seemed comfortable with each other. I'm surprised."

"What about you? Are you single these days?"

"I am currently unattached," Jessica announced with a grin.

The relentless snowflakes were blanketing the car. The front and rear windshields already had a thin layer of powder and the passenger door windows weren't far behind. Through a small clear patch, I looked out at the great lawn which had transformed into a sea of white shadows. The Trinity campus was deserted.

"Cozy in here," Jessica said.

"It's like we're in an igloo," I said.

"You don't mind if I take them off. They're kinda tight on me." Jessica started pulling on her left boot. Having trouble with it, she lifted her leg up in the air. I held the heel steady while she slid her foot out then helped her with the other one. Jessica propped up her bare feet on the right corner of the dashboard and nestled her head over and onto my lap.

"Good thing I don't have a stick," I said.

"Sure you do," she smiled.

"Now, now," I said. "Settle down."

Jessica placed her hand on my cheek.

"Your eyes were watery at the end."

"Give me a break," I said. "Barely."

I didn't care. It was true my eyes had welled up in the final minutes of the movie when the couple crashed their car on a wet country road after finally finding happiness. I had already accepted the fact that my threshold for tears had dropped over the last three months to make up for the ten years prior.

"I like that," Jessica said looking up at me. "I like guys who aren't embarrassed about expressing their emotions. That's attractive."

"I guess," I said. "No, actually I don't guess. I agree. It's nice expressing how you feel."

"Take off your clothes," Jessica giggled.

We both laughed. Daniel Day Lewis wasn't subtle when his character used the line in the movie, but he had his way with the women every time.

"You know I envy you," I said. "You're so relaxed in your life, so carefree. I'm jealous. I wish I had more of that."

"Stick with me, kid."

Jessica adjusted her head and shoulders either to get more comfortable or to arouse me.

"No, honestly, I think you have so much going for you. Any guy would be very, very lucky to have you."

I couldn't see out any more. The car was buried. It was only the two of us.

"Maybe one day you can tell me your secret-," I added, "the secret to your tranquility."

"I can tell you right now if you wanna know."

"Go ahead."

"Do you listen to Queen?"

"I know their songs," I said.

"*Nothing really matters... anyone can see... nothing really matters... nothing really matters to me.*"

Jessica sang the lyrics with a sweet, sexy voice. She saw me staring at her lips and pulled me in for a kiss. For the first time in a month, I felt wonderfully relaxed. We took our coats off and made out for the next fifteen minutes. When I thought she might be getting uncomfortable in the car and ready to go inside, Jessica proved me wrong by climbing onto my lap. She cupped my cheeks with all her fingertips and kissed my mouth in slow motion. I untucked her turtleneck and reached under it with both hands stroking her all the way up to her supple neck.

Jessica's head dropped back, and she let out a throaty moan through a gaping mouth. Any mutual gratification was over, her own needs suddenly intensified. She reached for the lever and dropped my seat back. She undid my belt and unfastened all five buttons on my jeans with a single forceful tug. I lifted my behind trying to keep up, as she yanked my jeans and underwear down below my knees before cramming them into a ball with the soles of her feet. Splaying out her skirt to cover my lower half, she rested her pelvis on mine. I found out that a long, demure garment doesn't always imply a conservative nature as Jessica had nothing on underneath. Stretching her left arm behind her back, she reached under her skirt and took the initiative. It was lost then and there, as she bit her bottom lip and began wiggling forward and back.

"Don't."

She saw it in my face.

"Don't," she repeated. "No. Don't."

I fought the battle for all of eight seconds before willingly surrendering when defeat had become imminent.

****

Jessica and I were bundled up again when we exited the car and made our way through untouched snow to the dormitory lobby. The warmth of the foyer was soothing as we came in from the blustery chill and stomped the powder off our shoes. An antique pendulum clock which hadn't been working all semester chimed. It was precisely two in the morning when we turned towards the hallway leading to the stairs.

Three bodies speaking at the top of their voices and laughing rambunctiously were slouched on the floor leaning against the hallway wall. Two were men my age- one black-bearded in torn jeans, the other with skinny tattooed arms and combat boots. I didn't recognize either. Between them sat Cybill, which I found strange since she didn't live at Galen Hall. All three looked worn-out and intoxicated. Each held a beverage wrapped in a brown paper bag, and although none were smoking, the hallway reeked of pot.

The group became curiously quiet as Jessica and I walked carefully past each pair of outstretched legs. The calm barely lasted. As soon as we were by, Cybill burst out laughing hysterically. Jessica kept moving, but I slowed to glance back. Cybill flicked her black hair over to the side and stared straight at me with glowing green eyes- color contacts for sure since I knew her eyes were naturally brown. She was pointing at us, which drew me to a halt.

Jessica noticed Cybill's gesture and grabbed my arm.

"Let's go upstairs," Jessica said.

I held my ground. We were ten feet from the group. Cybill was still aiming her index finger in our direction, her deep emerald glare piercing through me. In a loud but composed voice, she spoke: "You're gonna die. You were right but you were wrong. I see it. You're gonna die."

"Is she talking to me?" Jessica said.

I didn't answer. I didn't know.

"Christianity killed Epicurus," Cybill said. "Dintcha do the reading?"

Jessica gave me an inquisitive glance.

"She's stoned out of her mind," I said.

"I'd sleep it off if I were you," Jessica said to Cybill. "You look pretty awful."

The two men started laughing. Cybill's previously unruffled expression transformed to one of pure resentment.

"Whore," she said looking over at Jessica. "How many cars have you fucked in?"

Jessica was quiet. I thought she was going to cry.

Cybill looked back at me: "You *of all people* should know better than to hang around with this slut. She'll probably give you AIDS and shit."

"Let's go," I said and this time I pulled Jessica towards the stairs.

Before the heavy metal door retracted shut, I heard Cybill make one final attempt: "Christianity killed Epicurus."

Chapter 20

Jessica and I spent the night tightly nestled beside each other on my single bed. She slept in Victoria's Secret pink flannel pajamas which she brought from home, while I was in my boxers and a T-shirt. I gave her the inside and hovered near the edge of the bed unable to get comfortable. The late night altercation with Cybill had unsettled me, and I struggled to fall asleep. Glimmering specks of daylight had begun to penetrate the vertical blinds when I finally nodded off.

I woke up three hours later and looked over. Jessica was sitting up in bed with her eyes shut and her back up against the wall. The soles of her feet were pressing on each other, while her heels were pulled in towards her groin. She had her fingers wrapped perfectly around her toes except for a gap between her index and middle fingers through which my pill bottle stuck out like a fire hydrant.

Sensing my movement, she took one more deep breath in before opening her eyes.

"Good morning," she leaned over without fully breaching her pose and gave me a peck on the lips.

"Hi," I said staring at the bottle.

"It was under the sheets. I kicked it in my sleep."

I was wide-awake.

"You know what it is?" I asked.

"Anti-depressant?"

I sighed and took the bottle from her.

"Remember I told you I was going through a bad time?"

"Ty, you don't have to explain anything to me."

"It works, and it's a safe drug," I said, "and my liver's in good shape."

"What difference does that make?"

"Its side effects are on the liver- hepatitis."

"But how does hepatitis...?"

"I looked it up," I said. "It's like an inflammation of the liver from the drug."

"I thought it was from a virus."

"It's a wastebasket term," I said. "It also means an infection of the liver. I read about that too. There's 'A', 'B', and 'C'. Each letter stands for a different virus. 'A' you get by eating seafood or somebody's stool-you know, fecal-oral. 'B' and 'C' you get from drug needles or sex sorta like H.I.V. 'B''s less of a problem 'cause there's a vaccine for it. 'C''s more complicated because there's no vaccine."

I ran out of distraction. Jessica must have noticed my unease.

"I'll be right back," she said rolling over me on her way to the bathroom.

I was worried what she might be thinking. Then again, what did I know about her? Cybill's 'AIDS' comment scared me. Jessica probably did sleep around. It was certainly consistent with her unflustered, sexually aggressive personality. She routinely barged into the men's showers in Santorini. She asked me for my number in front of Miranda who she thought was my girlfriend at the time. And the way she laid out on the youth hostel roof wearing a string bottom and jiggling her breasts for attention. What was she doing in Santorini alone anyway? And for an entire summer? Probably screwing all the male tourists who were there for the sole purpose of finding a floozy like her to mess around with.

Jessica climbed back into bed. I could smell mint on her breath. She was hoping for an encore. She pulled me towards her and planted her lips on mine. I didn't kiss back.

"You OK?"

"No," I said. "I'm not."

My answer was tinged with anger.

"I'm sorry I found them," she said. "Ty, I don't judge people. I'm not in any position to judge people."

I know you're not.

Her eagerness to have sex with me was disturbing. The forceful way she stripped off my pants and grabbed me was entirely slutty. Cybill was right. I knew better. At the very least, I should have worn a condom.

Had Jessica just infected me with H.I.V.? Or hep C? Had I just made the biggest mistake of my life? I knew better! Why hadn't I worn a damn condom? Had I just made myself sick for a brief bout of sexual gratification? Had this whore just infected me?

"Ty, I'm OK with it. I'm sorry if it bothers you I found it. But you know I would respect your privacy."

She might even be pregnant. What if I got her pregnant? What then?

Why didn't I wear a condom? What was I thinking? Did I blow it? Did I just gut my whole life?

"You know," I said, "I'm a little annoyed."

"Ty. Stop! I said I'm sorry. I didn't mean to find it."

"No, I'm annoyed about something else. Why didn't we use a condom yesterday?"

Jessica didn't answer. This wasn't the attack she had been expecting.

"What if you get pregnant?" I said. "Are you trying to get pregnant?"

"I'm on the pill," she said as if problem solved.

"So what? That's not a hundred percent. You're smart. You work in a hospital."

"Don't worry. I wouldn't keep it."

"Are you joking? Are you fuckin' joking? How can you be so flippant about it? Have you ever been tested?"

"I don't like where you're going with this, Ty."

"Jess, *have* you?" I yelled.

"For what?" she yelled back.

"H.I.V.?"

"No. Have you?"

"I don't need to be."

"Why not?"

"I'm clean."

"So am I."

"Is that why you came over here without any panties on?"

Jessica bolted out of bed.

"I liked you, you jerk," she said.

"But you were hoping to get lucky. Now I know what kind of physical therapy you put out."

"Ty, I'm sorry. I need to leave."

"Don't be sorry."

"You're an absolute jerk."

"You're not gonna win this one- I'm right, you're wrong."

Jessica changed into street clothes. She put her hair in a ponytail glancing at the bathroom mirror from outside the door. I stayed in bed staring up at the flaking paint on the ceiling. She stuffed her gym bag, put her jacket on, and swung open the front door. Before walking out, she hesitated. She looked back. I ignored her. Jessica shut the door softly behind her.

****

I was still in bed two hours later. If I had gotten her pregnant, my life would never be the same. If she had given me H.I.V.- I couldn't even fathom it. My psyche regressed back to yesterday afternoon's frail state. I felt my face flush. My eyes welled up and my head bowed forward again and again as I began to sob uncontrollably. I reached for my pill bottle and swallowed one without water.

For the next three quarters of an hour, I cried feeling mildly better only when the tap ran dry. I brought something to write on over to the bed but couldn't focus. I had reached the breaking point where even drafting poetry- my channel for evacuating the toxic overflow- had become impossible.

From across the room, I spotted my hand-written Post-it note hanging on the refrigerator. It was too far for me to read but I knew the counsel well.

"What am I doing?" I said out loud. "What am I doing? This is my life. This is my one chance. I'm doing this all wrong!"

I shut my eyes tightly. *The tears need to stop. The tears must stop!* I had to lose the role of helpless victim. I needed to push myself to be pro-active. Happiness wasn't looking to entertain me. I had to search out happiness and *insert* it into my life. The painful feelings needed to go. The hopeless thoughts had to be flushed away. This was essential to begin to cleanse myself.

"Stop the crying and fix things!" I said.

But how? I knew to live for now. But my simply understanding this was no longer adequate. I had to execute as if I were abiding a sacred commandment.

I can find the strength. My parents were slated to arrive in New York later this week. Philip must have said something since they left a message on my machine saying how important it was for them to spend some quality time with me. Undoubtedly, their visit would be helpful. And since I also had my meds back, critical support would be available on two fronts.

Unfortunately, in the moment, I felt jittery and restless all the way down to my toes. I had to regain control. Now! Right away! With urgency!

How would Uncle Timos manage this kind of obstacle? How would he persevere if unwarranted anxieties and aberrant fears wreaked havoc on *his* soul? How would he answer if I asked him the age-old question: 'Uncle, how do you kill the Devil?'

I sprung out of bed. I put on yesterday's clothes, grabbed the pills, my keys and wallet, and rushed out the door. Conceivably, I had stumbled upon the path to a solution. More likely, the medication had reached a therapeutic level.

Chapter 21

I sped down I-95 South at 90 miles per hour weaving in and out of traffic, passing cars from the right when the fast lane wasn't moving fast enough. My mood had shot up like a missile. Things were good again. *I could do this.*

Despite an awful night's sleep, I wasn't tired. I knew what I had to get my hands on. I put the volume up and started singing to every stupid song that was playing butchering the lyrics and laughing out loud. Other drivers looking in must have imagined I was high. Truth is I was. My mind was moving faster than my thoughts.

I entered our apartment and shouted Philip's name but he wasn't home. My bedroom was exactly as I had left it. I took the pill bottle out of my pocket and dropped it into the bottom drawer of my desk. The komboloi was barely visible under a stack of paper and old letters. I brought it over to my childhood bed and lied down.

I had purposely left the komboloi behind when I moved to Hartford because of the upsetting memories it triggered. I had hoped to eradicate the distressing final image of Uncle Timos- the gruesome one plastered inside me- by storing away the visual cues. But now it was time to conjure up his memory again. He had prepared to be there for me even after his end.

I propped my head up on two pillows and got comfortable. I shut my eyes and ran the fourteen yellow beads between my fingers taking long drawn-out breaths in and out, in and out. A few minutes later, both my mind and body felt more relaxed. But this wasn't good enough. Something wasn't right. Something was missing. *What am I doing wrong?* I repeated the breathing exercises and this time tried to draw up happier memories.

What was it that my great-uncle had taught me about the komboloi? Repetitive activity reduces stress. But there had to be more to it. Perhaps a secret? Some hidden meaning? I opened my eyes and sat up. *Fourteen beads.* Did the number mean something? What could be fourteen? Fourteen challenges? Fourteen lessons? Fourteen rules?

Rules? Was it possible there were fourteen rules? Rules to live by? Rules by which to improve myself? I had formulated many new ideas since Uncle Timos' death. Maybe it was time I put them all together- first on paper then in practice. Was this the way out? Was this the road to recovery? Would this lead to my salvation? Could I elicit fourteen rules by which to make myself into a better human being?

I sat at my desk with the komboloi in front of me. The first one must have something to do with the *difficult truth-* the one which had preoccupied me these last few months. My opinion about the end was mildly off the beaten path, but I had never wavered from this core belief. I started writing. *1. Death is annihilation.* I had first suspected it when I sensed the void that was my great-uncle's corpse. Uncle Timos had ceased to exist- a fact which will remain valid for eternity. *A fact!* Having been exposed to some of the grim realities of life this last year, I was absolutely convinced. We each get our time and that's it. Some people can accept it. Most people can't. I pounded my fist on the desk. Rule one would serve as the foundation for the others.

Because of the difficult truth- a grim concept in our everyday reality- the emphasis had to be on living and on the 'now.' *2. Live for now.* This rule was something I had known and maintained all my life although I found it hard to put into practice as of late. I could have been the one killed in that accident. How instantaneously Uncle Timos had been deleted. Our existence was unpredictable. The emphasis must be on the present. As I stared at rule two, it seemed obvious. What's more, by failing to follow what is simple and straightforward common sense, I had caused one of my greatest regrets- not expressing to Miranda exactly how much she meant to me. The opportunities were there. Instead, I let two summers pass without revealing and demonstrating my full affection.

My leg was shaking under the desk. *Keep going!*

One of the keys to living a good life must include removing the inevitability of death from any list of fears. Uncle Timos hadn't flinched when Zoe waved her knife at his face. He wasn't afraid. Meanwhile, I was constantly terrified of not existing and this affected every aspect of my life. *3. Fearing death wastes precious time.* I remembered how completely distraught I was when Cybill flashed that tarot card at me. How many times over the last three months had I panicked thinking I had one or another of myriad illnesses. So many hours of my life- *my one and only life-* wasted worrying about dying. This had to stop! If- upon dying- the state of death won't concern me given rule one then why should I let it plague me during my brief period of life?

And what about God? How did He fit into all this? If there was a God- which more and more I didn't believe to be the case- He demonstrated very little interest in people. *4. God is indifferent about us.* Perhaps the reason no one will ever solve the problem of evil is that we simply can't accept the fact that God's moved on. Over the last few months, He had ample opportunities to pull me up and restore my faith, but instead He ignored my pain. What had I done to deserve retribution? I had been good all my life. I was being punished... for what exactly?

Yes, yes, yes, yes, yes!

How should I go about making the rest of *my* life fulfilling? Acquiring some level of power shouldn't necessarily make me 'bad' like Philip used to say, but I also didn't think the pursuit of it made for a good life. How much was enough? It's a limitless concept. Wielding power couldn't bring me peace of mind. Perhaps learning more about nature and my surroundings and appreciating the living beings all around me. But not power in and of itself and definitely not money! *5. Pursuing power or money won't lead to happiness.* The few things in life I deemed important were accessible to me even now- at a time when I was both weak and broke. After all, only a few months ago, I was sitting side by side with Miranda on the edge of a historic cliff admiring the universe and reflecting on how beautiful love was. I couldn't have been happier at that moment. I probably won't ever be as happy.

That's five. I had thought long hours about much of this over the last month. My great-uncle had known all along. He knew I'd figure it out. That's why he stressed the importance of the komboloi.

The rules will help me structure my thoughts. They'll allow me to arrange my beliefs so that I may stay true to them. They'll help me gather the strength I need to garner perspective. Number five steered me away from certain things. The next few needed to direct me towards something.

Not all forms of power are the same. Power as it pertained to knowledge should *not* be undesirable. If I had been more informed about depression, I would've diagnosed the signs and symptoms sooner and not have been plagued for months by painful thoughts and concerns over illnesses I never had. Uncle Timos was right about medicine. I must think seriously about becoming a doctor. *6. Learning about the world around us dispels our daily fears.* There were many ways to learn about the nature of the universe. Medicine would be my choice.

My mom and dad, Philip, Uncle Timos, Miranda, even Rob. How I missed them all. *7. Respect and cherish family and friends.* Thanks to my parents, I had always known this rule, but now it had to be included as a piece of a much larger puzzle.

What else did I need to do? How else could I be pro-active and change my life for the better? What about my current situation? The fact that I was searching for pleasure was natural. Everybody does across all ages, across time. I recalled Uncle Timos' words after handing me the komboloi and jotted down number eight. *8. Happiness must be sought.* And what about the bad times? Was there something to do with pain? Or maybe the avoidance of anguish and suffering? Nine would be an extension of eight. *9. Avoid pain at all costs.* I had suffered in one form or another for months. From now on, I would do everything I could to steer clear of it.

The pills might as well have given me hepatitis. My liver was failing in that I wasn't able to detox the poisons leaking out of my brain into my bloodstream and making me sick. Prometheus came to mind. Punished by the gods for delivering fire to man, he was chained to a cliff for eternity while an eagle flew in day after day pecking off pieces of his liver. The organ would regenerate only for the ritual to be repeated. The liver's ability to rebuild was nothing short of miraculous. I could revive my own tortured ψυχή and will myself back to wellness. *10. As long as there is life, there is time for change.* Uncle Timos believed he could fix even hardened criminals given the chance. I could undo the last few months of my life. I could come up with a strategy to climb out. I smiled- the remedy was already in my grasp.

There were more. I was missing four. But I had to stop now. I didn't want to force the rest. I shouldn't pretend to understand it all. I had time. The first ten had come easily but I needed more experience. With life! The final four could wait. There was ample time for each one of them to declare themselves.

I got up and stretched. I laughed out loud before jumping and slapping the ceiling.

"Time for my comeback! Regenerate, baby! Regenerate!"

I had formulated ten rules which I believed could lead me to the peace of mind I yearned for, ten principles which would help me find serenity and pleasure and regain a life without melancholy.

I see the finish line at the bottom of the hill. Go! From the corner of my eye, I see him running a few feet behind me. He's a shadow. Can't make out a face or anything. Can't even tell if he has any clothes on.

But this isn't a race. Now I understand. I have to stop him from crossing. Must slow down to grab hold of him. Whoever wins gains omnipotence.

But wait. I can't win. I can only prevent him from winning.

Large bushes near the bottom of the hill. It's not a racetrack any more. It's an obstacle course. Enormous lights over the stadium. The night is day. He's winding around the barriers so fast. I'm in front again… barely. Finish line's only a few feet ahead. I can win. But no, the goal is to stop him from crossing. Another opening. How does he zig-zag so quickly around those bushes?

He's ahead. He's crossing first. I've been beaten.

He's gone. It's quiet now. Racetrack lights are dimming, fading to black. Can't see much. Where did he go? All I can see is the stars. Stars were brighter earlier, but now they're dimming. It's getting darker, darker. Someone's turning off the stars.

Only thing I'm left with is… nothing at all.

I'm alone with my thoughts.

Tum…Fshhhhhhhhhhhhhhhh

Light. There's light. I see light.

Tum…Fshhhhhhhhhhhhhhhh

My mother. I can see my mother.

Tum…Fshhhhhhhhhhhhhhhh

My mother. Gasp. My mother.

"It's OK. We're still here. We're not going anywhere."

My mother.

Help me.

Part III

New York City, 1998 (continued)

Chapter 22

It was eight o'clock Saturday morning on one of those rare weekends I had completely off from work. Still in bed, I took my morning pill with a small sip from a water glass sitting on the floor.

Over the last few weeks, I had hoped to bump into Kelly around the hospital, but it never happened. I walked by the nephrology offices a dozen times, but except for a mailbox with her name on it, there was no sign of her. The only thing the departmental administrators could tell me was that she was 'in and out.' Certainly I could have paged her, but I didn't feel right calling her out of the blue to ask for Miranda's number. I preferred it to appear spontaneous.

I turned my pillow over and lied down on the cool side. I remembered Kelly's words from our chance encounter. If she had been precise and if the plan hadn't been altered, Miranda would be staying at her apartment in New York this weekend. What's more, I knew where Kelly lived which happened to be across the street from where I worked. No one would find my being in the area suspicious. I could definitely justify a fortuitous encounter.

****

Forty-five minutes later, I pulled in along the curb in front of Kelly's building. It wasn't a legal parking space on account of a hydrant, but I wasn't planning on leaving the car and the spot gave me a clear, unobstructed view of the lobby.

I put my sunglasses on and lowered both sun-visors. The streets and sidewalks were empty which wasn't surprising for a Saturday. If either Kelly or Miranda walked into or out of the building, I would easily spot them.

A full hour passed during which time I played with the radio dial compulsively pressing the 'search' button every time a song I didn't care for came on. I wiped grime off my sunglasses' lens. I picked up some trash from the floor of the car. A second hour went by. Through the rear view mirror, I looked across the street at the post-call doctors and nurses who were shuffling out of the hospital. I remained sufficiently incognito. I reclined my seat and opened the window a quarter of the way down to let in a gentle breeze. I yawned more than once. A third hour passed. I thought about Miranda and what I would say to her after so long. I closed my eyes only for a moment.

****

Tap, tap, tap.

A knock on the passenger's side window. A woman's torso. A delicate hand with long red fingernails reaching for the handle. Miranda stepped inside and shut the door.

"I don't believe it," I said.

Miranda hugged me. She looked exactly as I remembered.

"Ty, I've really missed you."

"You'll never believe how much I've missed you."

She kissed me softly on the lips.

"Does it go back any more?" she said.

Although my seat was already reclined, I dropped it down as far as it would go.

"Close them, Ty. I just want you to enjoy it."

I shut my eyes and covered them with my knuckles.

"I've wanted to do this for you for a long time," she said unfastening my belt.

Miranda wrapped her left hand around both my index fingers and pulled my forearms above my head lightly restraining me. She was gentle and tender. I let out a slow deep sigh. The trust I felt with her *there* made my whole body go numb, completely numb.

****

I woke up midway through the orgasm and instantly felt like a complete jackass. The sun was in a different place. The digital panel read after two in the afternoon. I moved my seat up and looked out the window. Kelly was across the street in her scrubs walking in my direction. She had a mobile phone pressed up against her ear and looked downtown before beginning a slow jog across the avenue.

I looked down at my lap relieved by my choice of thick denim and nonchalantly stepped out of the car.

Kelly saw me. I smiled back.

"You won't believe who's standing directly in front of me," Kelly spoke into her mobile. "Let's see how long it takes you to figure it out."

She handed me the phone.

"Hello," I said certain of who was on the other end.

"Who's this?" said the sweetest voice.

"This is Ty."

"Ty! I don't believe it," Miranda said. "What a blast from the past! How are you?"

"I'm doing well, very well. Are you in town?"

"How'd you know? The weather's so nice. I'm in the park."

"Central Park?"

"Yeah."

"What are you doing… rest of the day?" I said.

"That's what we were just talking about," Kelly said as she stood next to me by the curb. "I'm on call and I have to get back in a little bit. Today was not supposed to be this busy."

A cluster of taxis accelerated down First Avenue, and I couldn't hear Miranda for a few seconds. Luckily, I caught the tail end: "…but I have no major plans."

"Not only that," Kelly added, "but I have to take my son to a birthday party later." She leaned in and yelled into the phone, "Sorry, Randy."

"Tell her it's OK," Miranda said.

"Don't worry about it… from Miranda," I said. "Miranda, I can keep you company. I'd love to see you. Do you want to meet up… even now? I can find you in the park."

"I'm near the Boathouse," she said.

"I can meet you there. By the bar on the left," I said. "Is that OK with you, Kelly, if I entertain?"

Kelly nodded.

"I just need to drop something off at my apartment real quick," I said, "and then I'll come find you. Let's say an hour from now at the Boathouse?"

I was not going to let an adolescent wet diaper stand in the way of a perfect reunion.

Chapter 23

A blue sky over the city rained down hope. I avoided more than a few cyclists, rollerbladers, and joggers while trekking through the park's main path towards the Boathouse Restaurant. I was comfortable in baggy jeans, a white button-down shirt and penny loafers.

Through the restaurant's side-gate railing, I could see that every table in the outdoor seating area was occupied- not surprising for an unseasonably warm early October afternoon. Situated beside the dining room balcony and open-air bar, the lake was saturated with wooden rowboats casually being paddled without destinations.

As I browsed the diverse assortment of faces scattered along the porch, my gaze settled on a young lady sitting alone with her back to me. She wore a short black dress and sat femininely with her long legs crossed and nearly crossed again. A glass of wine sparkled on the circular metal table in front of her. I saw her turn and look towards the entrance. Her hair was cut short in the back, while large black sunglasses covered her face. She sipped her wine before removing her sunglasses and placing them down. It was Miranda. She was a woman.

My heart was suddenly pounding as a tremendous sense of déjà vu came over me. This persona was a familiar one- an image forever etched in my mind. Miranda had not simply grown up, she had transformed. I had predicted this metamorphosis and it was now complete. I knew it was totally irrational, but unlike everything else in my life, *this* absurdity I wasn't going to cleanse with reason. Instead I would enjoy the improbable fact that today I would be meeting 'ma femme fatale.'

I jogged around the fence and into the restaurant.

"You look fan-tastic!" I said arriving at her table.

"TY!"

Miranda jumped out of her seat and gave me a hug. I didn't have to look around to know that she was the most beautiful woman in the restaurant.

"*You* are in business school? Are you crazy? Have you thought about modeling?" I raised both my hands palm side up as if to say 'Just look at you!'

"I'm a little taller than you remember, huh?" she laughed.

"Sit, please. Tell me about life in D.C." I pulled a chair up and was momentarily distracted by a pack of Marlboro's between her wine glass and purse.

"Oh, I lo-o-o-ove Washington. Have you been?" she said.

"Long time ago."

"It's a great town, and I'm having a really good time. Of course, San Fran is still my first choice. And you? You've been in New York the whole time?"

"For the most part, believe it or not, I have- except for college. Where'd you end up?"

"U.S.F.- I stayed near home," she said. "Ty, whatever happened to 24, 26, 28? You were supposed to have things all mapped out."

"I don't believe you remembered- my Porsche, my million and my wife, right?"

"Yeah," she giggled. "So what happened?"

"Well, I drive a leased Toyota. I'm about a million dollars shy of my goal- actually, I owe people money from all my student loans. And as for marriage, well let's just say I have yet to introduce my parents to a serious girlfriend so right about now they're probably thinking I'm gay."

"Are you?" Miranda's tone made her question seem legitimate.

"No, I'm not gay. I'm just busy."

"You're not gay. You're just busy," she repeated. "I don't know, Ty. Sounds like an admission to me." She giggled while reaching for her sunglasses.

"How much have you had?"

"First glass. C'mon, you know I'm kidding." Miranda crossed her legs again tugging forcibly at the bottom of her dress but failing to cover the brawny thigh now exposed.

"I guess the 24, 26, 28 didn't really work out the way I planned. Most people- I guess including myself before I went through all this- most people have a real misconception about medicine. They think all doctors must make lots of money, but they forget the four years of college, followed by four years of med school, followed by four to nine years of residencies and fellowships during which time we make minimum wage for the hours we work and by the time we finish we're in our mid-thirties. Anyway, at least for me, it's not about the money."

"I wouldn't have thought you'd be any other way," she said.

Miranda sipped her wine and caught me peeking at her thigh. I quickly turned my head and looked out over the lake only to be blinded by the sunlight reflecting off the water. I felt her hand push down on my knee: "Stop shaking, Ty. You're making me nervous."

"Sorry," I said.

"Kelly says you wanna be a surgeon? What kinda surgeon?"

"I'm not sure yet. I like a few things."

I remembered a distant conversation and wondered if she did as well. Meanwhile, some guy from the next table kept looking over at Miranda, which was rude and surprising since there was a woman sitting across from him. I didn't care. I even liked it. She was with me.

"So why surgery?"

I smiled. I always had fun with this question.

"Possibly because I'm selfish, and I wanna get comfortable with bad disease to take the edge off."

"What the heck does that mean?" she said fighting with her dress some more.

"...or possibly because there was a time when I was obsessed with my own mortality and wanted to get better acquainted with the premise of death and dying...or possibly because of the challenge of it all...or possibly because I just like to cut people open..."

"Yuck!"

"...or possibly because I want to spend my days sitting on the ledge of a cliff, enjoying the breathtaking view and *catching* anybody who wanders over the edge."

Miranda tapped my knee with her knuckle twice. "You're doing it again."

The waitress took our order. I asked for a glass of Chardonnay. Miranda asked for an ashtray. We decided to split the shrimp cocktail.

"So do you get a lot of time off?" she said reaching for a cigarette and hanging it from her lips. "It must be tough with your hours."

"I wish I had more time to travel but I don't," I said. "Have you been back to Greece at all?"

"Not in a while- not since my mom got sick." Miranda stroked her lighter and lit the cigarette squinting her eyes as she inhaled. "I'm going to Paris next week," she blurted out along with smoke, "just for three nights, but that's alright, maybe I'll have some interesting gossip for you when I get back."

"Like what?" I said.

She winked at me through her sunglasses.

"Ty, I knew you'd get where you are. I knew you'd do well. I was sure of it."

"I've done alright. You know there was a time- I'll call it my blue period- when things were rough. I was just unhappy. Nothing made me happy. It was just a really bad time for me."

"Everybody goes through something like that at some point. I did. You get into problems when you don't talk about it. Once you let it out, it gets better. Hey, you still write poems?"

"Funny you should mention it since I just finished one, but rarely."

"Why not? I loved your poems. Send me one. Put it in a letter and send it to me like you used to. You know I still have your old letters." She hesitated. "I keep all that kinda stuff. It's nice to reminisce once in a while." Miranda rubbed my forearm affectionately as if she were petting a dog.

"Why'd we lose touch?" I asked.

She blew out some more smoke as a woman's arm reached in with an ashtray. "I don't know. We were kids- at least I was a kid. I've grown up a lot since then." She set down her cigarette and brushed her hair back with both hands before letting it settle evenly along the sides of her face. "I don't know, but it's in the past, right?" She leaned back on her chair extending her legs until they found their way between my own. Miranda removed her sunglasses. "So tell me what's going on, you know, in your personal life. Any young women I should be jealous of?"

"Here and there," I stuttered as the waitress balanced my wineglass on a napkin. "Nothing serious, really…nothing…" My hand reached for the glass and muzzled me with a sip.

"Ty, your leg."

"Sorry."

"Why not?" Miranda maintained a steady gaze. Her big eyes opened wide.

"It's tough," I said. I felt her leg make gentle contact with my own. "I mean, I date, but I haven't been looking for anything- anybody- serious… for a serious relationship." I searched all around her glare for a safe place but couldn't fine one. "I'm just too busy."

A different waitress set down a glass of red wine on our table.

"I don't think we ordered…," I said.

"From the gentlemen," she replied pointing to the table directly behind me.

I spun around. Four dark-haired men laughing disorderly on account of two empty bottles on their table had their glasses raised high above their heads aimed in our direction. I had been so focused on Miranda that I hadn't noticed them before then.

"I don't think it's for me," I said to Miranda.

"Cheers," they slurred one after the other.

Miranda drank from their gift.

"And thank you very much," one of them added, "you know, for the view."

I made nothing of the comment until I saw Miranda put down the glass, bounce up from her reclined position and vigorously pull down on her dress.

"Your smile. He means your smile," another one blurted followed by a guffaw.

Miranda put her sunglasses back on and turned away. Her cheeks and neck were flushed

I looked at the rowboats only to be blinded again.

"It's not always easy being attractive," I said.

Miranda didn't reply. Fortunately, the group got up and left. One thing's for sure- they weren't Italian.

A platter of jumbo shrimp over a thin layer of crushed ice arrived in time to help change the mood. Miranda stamped out her cigarette, and we attacked the shrimp bowl in unison making short work of the small jar of cocktail sauce. She tried again to push the conversation to personal matters while I continued to sidestep the topic. I'm sure Miranda expected me to ask questions about her own past relationships, but I didn't want to know any of it. That entire period was gone, irretrievable. I didn't care. And I knew it would hurt.

"I'm sorry about your mother," I said, "but you smoke?"

"Ty, don't play doctor with me."

"You know that wonderful feeling of indestructibility we all have when we're young," I said. "I lost it a while ago when I was still in college. But things are going well for you. It hasn't been taken from you yet."

"Ty, you thought *I* was the one who's been drinking," she laughed.

"So what do you think the point of all this is?" I said.

"Point of what?"

"Life," I answered expecting her to have understood. "Some people think the whole point is to enjoy it. Every single second of it.

Live for now. The important things in life are right there in front of us."

Miranda pointed at me then back at herself. "Directly in front of us?"

"Of course," I said reeled in by her playful tone.

"Attractive?" she asked with a serious look on her face.

"Very."

Miranda picked up the last shrimp and hung it in front of my mouth. I gladly bit into it.

"So if we're supposed to live for now then why shouldn't I smoke? It makes me happy. Ty," Miranda pinched my forearm, "would you ask me to do something that might compromise my happiness?"

"No, but I want you to live a long life so I really hope you quit."

Miranda lit another cigarette.

"So if the point of life is just to enjoy it, isn't that a bit selfish?" she said. "Just looking out for your own personal pleasure?"

"It depends," I said. "If all you get is eighty or so years, assuming you're lucky, then loving every bit of every day makes sense. If you tip the balance to being happy, maybe you're better off, more successful. I mean, if there isn't anything else and death's the end, well, it makes sense to avoid pain, max out on pleasure- doesn't it? Otherwise, we've failed."

"I hope you're not saying that it's better to just sit around and be drunk and stoned all the time- both of those things make lots of people happy like those jerks who just left. Because if that is what you're saying, you haven't exactly practiced what you're preaching. You spent all this time in school working, studying, trying to…"

"No, actually, that all works into it," I said. "If you figure out why things are the way they are, you get more comfortable with everything and you get rid of all your superstitions. Medicine helped me do that. I'm better off now than I used to be. And I hope you understand that when I say *searching for pleasure*, I'm implying something a bit more sophisticated than drugs and orgies."

"But only if you're right about one important thing." Miranda removed her sunglasses and fogged both lens with a series of warm breaths before wiping them with a napkin. "That this is our one life. Because if it's not, then your theory doesn't work any more. It doesn't hold water because you just end up wasting a lot of time running around looking for people to have sex with and any other quick thrill you can manage and- I don't know- probably ending up selfish and alone." She continued to fidget with her glasses. "Maybe this life is just a really small portion of a much broader…you know…"

"Journey," I said. "But for that to be the case, you must think that there's a god who actually cares about us. I'm not sure I buy it. At least I don't feel particularly cared for."

"There's more than this. There has to be."

"I'm not as optimistic," I said. "Think about it- do you really believe God cares about any of us?"

"I like my life. I do think He cares." Miranda began digging through her purse to find her ringing mobile phone. "Hello…Where are you?...Still?...You're kidding." She continued in Italian and turned her body towards the lake.

I stared at her. There was no rush. I didn't want to overwhelm her. Eventually she would come around. I looked deeper and began a meticulous dissection- the three barely-visible, linear creases running across her forehead, the paleness of her skin, the thin blue veins arborizing over her left temple, her dense sharply-groomed eyebrows, her uncolored and increasingly dry lips, her lean naughty neck, her prominent collarbones, the sprinkling of tiny moles over her breast bone. I snuck an unsatisfying glimpse at her small chest before reflexively transitioning into a full upper body stretch.

"That was Kelly," she said. "Our plans for tonight have completely fallen apart. The baby's going crazy, and the hospital's beeping her every ten minutes." She shook her head. "What d'you think? Do you want to do something with me tonight? Movie maybe? We're in New York. We can do anything, right? Maybe a play?"

"Phantom!" I said. "I'll see it again."

"And I'll see it for the first time. Will we find tickets? It's almost 6:30."

"Would you believe me if I told you I haven't heard that music since I last saw you?"

****

Although there weren't any seats available when we arrived at the theater, Miranda and I were fortunate in that there were a few no-shows. Ten minutes before curtains, we had two rear mezzanine tickets in hand.

The show was spectacular- much better than I remembered. When they sang *All I Ask of You*, I glanced at Miranda wondering what thoughts might be resurfacing.

Afterwards, we stepped out into a pleasant evening.

"You understand why he gave her up?" I asked. "He loved her so much that he would rather she be happy with someone else than be unhappy with him, but since *he'll* never be happy with anyone else, he vanishes."

"Are you sure you won't let me pay for my own ticket, Ty?"

My silence was answer enough.

We decided to walk the twenty city blocks to Kelly's East Side apartment. Inspired by the passion in the music, I reached down and took hold of Miranda's hand. I could even make out some stars glimmering faintly between skyscrapers. *This* was the point of it all.

"The purest love is the unselfish type," I said. "That's why I love this show. I'm drawn into the tragedy of it all. But that's the way it is- the best love stories are the ones where you have two people who really desperately want to be together but for one reason or another they just can't make it happen."

"Except I don't think she ever wanted to be with him in the first place," Miranda said, "whether he taught her music or not. I guess someone finally told the Phantom: 'Give it up. It's all in your head. She's not interested.'"

"But the bottom line is his love was sincere."

"Probably, but his life was one big delusion."

As we turned the corner to Kelly's apartment building, Miranda weakened her grip and let her hand fall away from mine.

"So will I see you tomorrow?" I said.

"Tomorrow may be tough," she said. "I've barely seen Kelly at all, and I'm sure she wants to see me. Then I have to catch the train to D.C."

"What about a quick dinner between the time you leave Kelly's and the train?" I stopped and faced her. "I just have to see you- whatever you can do. I have to see you once more before you leave."

"It's tight."

"A quick dinner."

"A quick dinner?"

"Fantastic." I clapped my hands. "I just want you to know even though we lost touch all these years, you're someone I consider very special."

I got her to smile.

"Ty, friends like you are hard to find," Miranda said. "Don't ever change on me." She kissed me on both cheeks before disappearing into the lobby.

I started walking uptown on First Avenue glancing over my shoulder for a cab home. Half a block later, a deep burning on my right side made me slow my pace. I stopped to press on my abdomen. Bright yellow lights turned blood red as the traffic whizzed by. It was late. It was dark. Miranda's re-emergence had served as a marvelous distraction, but I was alone again. Alone with my thoughts. I could feel it simmering. And this pain was on my right- the side of the liver. It had been over four weeks since I cut myself.

Please, please, not now.

Chapter 24

My parents had preserved a small portion of Uncle Timos' vast book collection after air shipping it to New York from London. Our living room housed two full shelves of this dispensed enlightenment including works on philosophy, psychology, and medicine, many of which I had read in their entirety. I woke up feeling better the next morning and spent most of the afternoon on the couch reviewing the day before, periodically leafing through tomes between daydreams and longing for evening to arrive.

Ominous rain clouds had begun their offensive over the city as I walked into Casa, a Moroccan place in Hell's Kitchen. Thick drapes let little light in, while prints of nude and semi-nude women lined the mirrored walls around the bar. In the back, sheer white curtains stylishly enveloped two dozen legless tables providing patrons with a modest privacy. Colorful pillows surrounding each table served as seat cushions for the dimly-lit dining room.

Miranda arrived a few minutes late with a high school knapsack hanging off one shoulder. She wore low-riding blue jeans and a white T-shirt- nothing special although every pair of eyes in the restaurant felt the urge to scan her up and down, half with envy, half with thirst. The maitre d' led us to the far end where mostly couples sat cocooned within drawn curtains. Miranda and I eased into the soft cushions settling next to each other cross-legged.

The waitress took our order before wittingly drawing the draperies shut and isolating us within our tiny space. A scented hummus arrived with warm bread in a spicy pepper sauce followed by a rich Cornish hen. Miranda eased into the appetizers confidently moving her hands around the table, caressing the food with her long fingers. Much more restrained, I scattered breadcrumbs all over me and succeeded in tipping over the wooden salt shaker. Once our entrees arrived, I cut a piece of my lamb and floated my fork up in front of her. She hesitated momentarily then leaned in and parted her lips allowing me in. Her pursed mouth circled in slow, arousing rotations.

"Well?" I asked.

Her eyes were smiling as her gaze made the involuntary trek up towards the ceiling.

"It's OK," she said.

She reached for her glass and sipped Bordeaux.

"Just OK?"

"It's OK," she repeated.

For dessert, I winded down with a rich, dripping Baklava trickling honey onto the napkin on my lap, while Miranda settled on a blood orange sorbet. She asked me if I wanted to try it but I wasn't in the mood for anything cold.

Throughout the meal, we reminisced about the islands, the beaches, and the good times we had over two fabulous summers. Every detail was clear in my mind, although most of my thoughts I kept buried- how her company made my breathing quicken, how her stare made me look away and lose my train of thought, how her absence made me close my eyes and recreate our time together.

Only after the waitress asked us if we wanted to order a second did I realize that we had sipped our way through a bottle of wine.

"Ty, those boxers you wore in the pool that night- where the heck did you get them? They had like tiny hearts all over them, didn't they? Did you buy them yourself?"

"I'm embarrassed to say I did."

"They were ridiculous," Miranda laughed.

"And I'm very happy to have had the opportunity to showcase them to your mother."

"You know after you got them wet, they were practically completely see- through."

"Well, that's great. Pour more salt on my wound. Next time, you get in the water with your underwear, and I'll call my parents over to say hello."

"That should be fun especially since I wear a thong."

Miranda pulled up her shirt. Her low-riding jeans only covered the bottom half of the red lace trim. *If confidence had a color, it would be red.*

"I can't understand how you women find those things comfortable," I said staring at the tantalizing island of skin between the side of her thong and her jeans.

Miranda pulled up on the strap with some force yanking it in my direction as far as it would go without tearing.

"Trust me," she said. "This feels really good. It's extremely comfortable, and as a woman, it makes me feel very, very sexy."

"What did you do to your little omphalos," I said noticing her pierced navel.

Burrowing her knees into the pillow, Miranda sat up and faced me. She raised her T-shirt all the way to her bra exposing every inch of her abs. A small gold ring perforated the upper surface of her bellybutton fold.

"Go ahead," she said. "Go ahead."

I grasped the ring between my thumb and index finger and gave it a gentle tug. *The omphalos, the beautiful omphalos.* How ironic- the center of my own universe displaying this symbol to me!

Miranda grabbed my hand and brought it to her lap.

"What does that say?" she said.

I had written the word 'αταραξία' in small-print red ink on the back of my hand.

"It says 'ataraxia,'" I said, "in Greek."

"What does that mean?"

"It's the only word I could find pretty much in any language that sums up what I feel when I have you next to me."

"Flattery will get you everywhere, Dr. Karos," Miranda tossed my hand away, "assuming it means something good."

"It's hard to define. Let's just say that if you can find ataraxia then your life was a success."

"Happiness," she said.

"Sort of. Not exactly."

"Ty, how is it that you've had so much time-off this weekend? I thought you residents were always strapped for time."

"We are. Your timing happened to be perfect. And every year of residency, it gets a little better. But I try and make time for me- sometimes even at the expense of sleep. I mean it's not just about the work. It should never be just about the work."

"The reason we work in the first place is to make time to enjoy life. Right?"

"Exactly!" I said. "And *this* is what it's all about! Tell me that's not the case."

"What do you mean 'this'?"

"Think about it," I said. "You work and work and work day in and day out, and nobody- really nobody- cares, *really* cares, about what you're feeling. Most of us are expendable, easily replaceable. Every so often, you have to stop everything, regain perspective. *This* is what it's all about, not work, not money. *This*- enjoying a wonderful evening with tasty food next to somebody you find incredibly interesting. Everybody works for the same reason- to make that little bit of money to get a place near the water so we can listen to the waves crashing on the beach while we're lying in bed next to that person we love."

Miranda rested her leg up against mine then glanced at me innocently as if nothing had happened. She continued to stare- her curvy eyelashes rising and falling in a slow, flowing rhythm- gazing all along the side of my face and neck. Her wandering glare finally came to a standstill at my lips! Miranda leaned in as if she wanted to tell me something.

"What?" I whispered.

She smiled shyly then reached up and stroked my cheek with her fingers. I drifted towards her in submission but quickly pulled back. Was I infected? Could I transmit it to her? Impossible if I hadn't converted. Unlikely in the minuscule chance that I had. But I didn't know and I couldn't be certain the chances were absolutely zero.

Our shoulders were resting up against one another in our miniature private room. The impulse was forbiddingly intense. Could one kiss possibly hurt? *I was without a Pythia.* I couldn't tell her what I was afraid of- how would she react to the news? I craved her but the stakes were too high. This was my little Miranda.

****

We cabbed it to Penn Station in the rain parting ways inside the terminal with a simple peck on each cheek. As Miranda walked away, I uttered a subdued, under-my-breath 'I love you' in her direction. Meanwhile, I prepared to experience the full wrath of my depression, which by now was yearning to make a stand. I knew the next few hours and days would be cruel to me.

A hooded homeless man passed me. Although I didn't get a good look at his face, he instantly caught my attention. Wearing tattered clothing with visible undergarments, he was drenched by the rain. I stopped and looked behind me. He was walking at a moderate pace in

Miranda's direction- maybe thirty yards behind her along a long passageway leading to the trains.

A sudden panic came over me. Might he rob her? Or worse, hurt her? Rape her? I watched him maintain his stride, while Miranda slowed her own pace and placed her mobile phone up against her ear. I followed them.

Miranda turned the corner onto the platform. I didn't want her to see me, but I wasn't about to back off from the suspicious character either. The vagrant followed her onto the same rail platform. I was now only a few yards behind him and made the same bend. The train was parked in the station. I was reassured by the fact that Miranda was nowhere to be seen- she must have boarded.

The homeless man stood on the platform mumbling to himself. I walked alongside the train- somewhat more leisurely now- and looked in through the windows to see whether I could spot Miranda. I scanned four or five cars before the doors abruptly shut. A minute later, the train pulled away.

I sat on a filthy wooden bench and took a deep breath. Finally at a standstill, I began to appreciate a strange new awareness gradually assaulting me. My face felt warm and flushed. A painful burning was spreading through my entire body as if I were being pummeled with hot steam. This was accompanied by a sudden, ferocious nausea. I glanced all around the empty platform, gagged and vomited charcoal-colored syrupy fluid directly onto the pavement between my legs. This was followed by a second wave and then a third. When I had no more to let out, a sudden terror came over me. Everything was about to come to an end. I stroked my hair back with both hands and found mounds of strands between my fingers. Tears started running down my cheeks uncontrollably as I listened to myself cry.

When I regained my bearings, I noticed a dark silhouette sitting next to me on the bench. I made every effort to avoid eye contact with the vagrant but kept watch over his shadowy figure from the corner of my eye. He was looking down at the tiled floor.

"Black bile," he said in a deep voice referring to the emesis at my feet. "You'll feel better once you get it all out." He put his arm up on the side of the bench. "It's funny," he laughed and followed with a smoker's cough, "you look at me and then you look at you, and I'd say I'm doing better than you today- funny how things have a way of even'n out."

No words would come. I felt as if an invisible hand was suffocating me. Everything was coming apart. A screeching noise grew louder and louder, and the station was suddenly illuminated by an incoming train.

"Hey man, there's no reason to go at it alone," the vagrant raised his voice to compensate for the shrill. "When things go bad, remember," he shouted pointing forward with his chin, "the way out's right in front of you."

The train barreled into the station. I bolted upright and started walking towards the street. Before picking up my pace, I took a quick glance back at the drifter only to find myself staring directly into the depths of my great-uncle's dead eyes.

Chapter 25

After I got home, I felt no better. The same achy abdominal pain from the night before returned. I couldn't sit. I needed to keep moving. I knocked on Philip's door, but he wasn't home. After years of progress, a decade of positive changes, I had come full circle. I was weak and pathetic. I flipped open the cap on my pill box and took an extra dose.

I couldn't sleep and felt even worse Monday morning retching between my bed and the toilet. For the first time since med school, I called in sick. When Ted asked me what the problem was, I said food poisoning without hesitating. I spent much of the afternoon in bed watching a moth circling the ceiling. I wasn't hungry so I pushed myself to eat plain bread and later some crackers. This only exacerbated my nausea and I vomited.

Tuesday morning, a ringing telephone woke me at dawn. Philip was calling from Boston. He had gone Sunday to visit a friend. He was up and figured I'd be awake getting ready to leave for the hospital. I told him I hadn't been well but planned to go in, but my optimism proved short-lived. A few minutes after drinking a tall glass of water to re-hydrate, I rushed to the toilet again but this time with diarrhea. I called in sick for a second day.

While in bed, I performed physical examinations on myself. My pulse was consistently a few beats above the high end of normal. My forehead felt a little warm but didn't burn enough to suggest a fever. I couldn't find a thermometer to confirm it either way. My abdomen was moderately distended, and although I continued to feel a vague right-sided discomfort, it was no longer a harsh pain. Pressing on my own belly didn't elicit significant tenderness, so I knew I didn't have an exam that warranted surgery. I was still losing strands of hair from the stress but fortunately less than the day before.

I was obliged to take a third day off when overnight on Tuesday I developed severe rigors which forced me to scamper out of bed and rummage for a second blanket. Throughout the day, I was tense and uneasy, feelings that waxed and waned but never completely receded. I continued to take my medication methodically. The pills were about the only thing I was able to keep down, popping one every morning and helping it down with a tiny sip. The one time I threw up a pill, I waited half an hour and swallowed a second.

For a fourth consecutive day, I didn't leave the apartment. I could barely get out of bed I felt so weak. Food wouldn't stay down so I didn't have a whole lot left in my gut to vomit. I forced myself to drink water. Even so, my mouth was dessert-sand dry. My urine grew darker and darker with each trip to the bathroom, while my urge to pee had fallen to only twice daily. My appointment with health services for the six-week hep C testing wasn't for another ten days. I reassured myself that I would get a general check-up then if these symptoms persisted.

On Friday, I woke up with a little more energy, even a sliver of optimism. I stayed in bed much of the morning daydreaming about Miranda. Finally, I gathered up the nerve to call her. I settled for her machine.

"Hi, it's me. I hate leaving messages, but I just wanted to let you know I'm thinking of you. Hope we can meet up again very soon. I'm sorry we haven't spoken more since the weekend. OK, well, I just wanted to say hello."

After I hung up, I remembered Miranda had asked me for a poem. From a shoebox in my closet, I removed a stack of papers of various sizes and textures- my poems, thirty-seven in all. I pulled out my komboloi and the red folder which contained my rules and set everything down on the bed. I scanned this collection- my most valuable items. I read the rules again one by one troubled that I was still missing two. I skimmed the poems reading bits and pieces of familiar text. Then, in clear hand-writing on a clean sheet of paper, I copied my most recent addition- the poem I had conceived while unwittingly observing Kelly's toddler running around a playground. I dropped it into an envelope and looked for a stamp, but a sudden intense bout of nausea forced me to rush to the toilet and retch.

After the episode relented, I stared into the bathroom mirror. My eyes were weary underscored by a dark purple. My hair was dirty and disheveled. The soft incandescent light blended with my skin distorting my complexion. I pulled off my T-shirt and ran my fingers along the depressions between my ribs. I felt so alone. I didn't deserve this. How can one person put up with so much? Nothing about this was fair. No surprise God was nowhere to be found. God had abandoned me long before I was born.

And where was Miranda? Why hadn't she called me? She could have at least phoned to thank me for dinner. Her views on life were off balance. She would have difficulty accepting the rules. She could at least *try* to see things a different way. I couldn't accept anyone thinking my rules were rubbish much less Miranda.

Perhaps I shouldn't send her anything. Who was she anyway? Just another pretty girl living a shallow life, men constantly ogling her, satisfying her every whim. Was this a life worth living? She was in no position to reject or even judge my way of thinking. I had accomplished much more with the rules than she ever would with or without them. Love and romance inevitably lead to vulnerability. My passion for Miranda made me weak. During both periods of my life when I was down, she had surfaced. Passion wasn't something anyone should live by. Passion was contrary to my beliefs and principles. Passion had once again disoriented me, made me lose perspective.

I grabbed the entire batch of poems and brought them into the kitchen. These poems represented my passion, their words merely symbols of emotions gone awry. I needed to rid my life of passion. From the drawer next to the sink, I pulled out a box of matches. I struck one and placed the flame under 'Thoughts in the Night.' A heavy black smoke was released and the paper was devoured in seconds. As soon as the heat reached my fingertips, I dropped the leaf and watched its charred remains float to the bottom of the sink. 'The Moment' was next. The poem had served its purpose. I had already incorporated its meaning into my rules. It was now expendable and so up in smoke it went.

I burned one poem after another until only a single sheet of paper was left. I lit this final leaf and watched it burn more radiantly than the others. When the flame reached my fingers, my eyes scanned the few remaining words near the bottom- *12. Life can hurt; death is painless.* I released the page and watched it float into the sink. The rules! I had burned the rules!

A high-pitched shrill pierced my eardrums. The smoke detector hung over the kitchen door inches from the ceiling. I jumped and punched the device with my fist, but it kept ringing. I tried again unsuccessfully. I leaped a third time, but I couldn't get it to stop. The room began to spin. I slid along the wall down to the floor and began to sob. *Please stop.*

"What the hell's burning?" Philip said hurling his backpack across the room.

He pulled a chair over, climbed on it and disconnected the entire unit from the wall. The battery dropped on the floor. The machine went silent, but I could still hear the ringing.

"What's going on? What's burning? Why are you crying?"

"I'm OK," I said looking up.

"Ty, your eyes are yellow. You're yellow."

"Yeah, I got hepatitis."

"So…what d'you have to do?"

"I gotta go to health services. I gotta get checked out," I said and stood up.

"Wait a minute!"

Philip placed his hand on my shoulder, but I pushed him aside. I put on my shoes and a T-shirt, grabbed my komboloi, and left the apartment.

****

It must have been around noon when I got off the 6 train at 28th street and walked four blocks to Brigham's employee health services. The nurse practitioner put down her sandwich and ushered me into an examination room. A minute later, the same doctor who had examined me on my first visit walked in and sat down across from me.

"You passed me in the hallway," he said scanning the skin on my face, neck, and arms. "You're jaundiced. Has no one told you how yellow you look?"

I looked at my hands turning them palm-side up then palm-side down.

"We'll get the hep C test done, but I'm sorry to say the diagnosis is pretty clear," he said. "You've converted."

I knew. I began to cry. I hoped he would say something positive, something to ease my pain.

"What were you thinking?" he said handing me a small box of tissues. "Why didn't you come in sooner?"

The room was at a tilt. I tried to recalibrate so as not to fall out of my chair.

"We need to admit you to the hospital," he said. "We need to confirm the virology. I want to check your liver function tests and get you re-hydrated. You don't look like you've been eating and drinking a whole lot?"

"Bread and water."

"That's not enough. Why didn't you come sooner?"

My depression now had legitimacy. I was exposed, vulnerable.

"And for how long have you been nauseated?" he said.

"All week."

"And you've been vomiting?"

"Every day."

"Fevers? Did you have fever?"

"Chills… I never checked."

The doctor pushed up my sleeve and Velcro-ed the blood pressure cuff on my right arm. I saw him glance at the komboloi in my other hand. Leaning in with a stethoscope, he pumped the bladder. I watched the mercury rise and fall. He ripped the cuff off shaking his head.

"Eighty-five over forty. I need to get you admitted."

"I can't."

"What do you mean? What could possibly be more important than your health?"

I'm not crazy. I walked out despite his efforts to convince me to reconsider and took the elevator down to the hospital's main lobby.

"Ty!" Philip jogged over to me. "There you are."

"He wants to put me in."

"Who does?"

"The doctor I just saw."

"Maybe he's right."

I dropped my head, defeated. "I'm afraid. I'm so afraid."

"Ty, you need to do the right thing. If they want you to stay the night, then stay. I'm here. You won't have to do this on your own. I'll help any way I can, so please let me. I'm your brother, and I love you."

****

Philip drew the curtain back a few notches and walked through. I was lying on an emergency department stretcher wearing only a ridiculous hospital gown. My clothes and my komboloi were in a plastic bag by my side.

"They let me through," he said. "The E.R.'s busy."

I reached over and took hold of Philip's hand.

A nurse had already placed an I.V. in my forearm and was administering the fourth liter of fluid into me. I had yet to sense the urge to urinate. A phlebotomist had also come by and drawn my blood for lab tests. Philip dropped to the floor next to my stretcher and we listened in silence to the unavoidable ruckus behind the curtain.

Ted Gorcki appeared.

"You doin' OK?" he said.

"Better."

"You wanna know your results?"

"Do I have a choice?"

He read from an index card: "Your lytes suggest you're extremely dehydrated- not surprising. Your bilirubin's seven. You're A.L.T. is 5,500. Your P.T.'s twenty. You let this go a bit, but you'll be OK. Sort of your classic presentation, you know, six weeks after exposure, you become nauseated and jaundiced. The hep C test is cooking, but you know what it's probably gonna show. But it'll all pass. You'll be a carrier. Nowadays with interferon and all these other new therapies, you'll be OK. Trust me. I had a good friend who got acute hep C, and he's had the virus for years, and he's doing fine. Trust me. Trust me."

I smiled. I had underestimated Ted. Ted Gorcki was humane.

Once an inpatient hospital bed opened up, they transferred me out of the emergency department up to a regular room. Philip had already informed our parents and must have painted a grisly picture since they made plans to be in New York the following evening.

The guilt began to set in. So many lives were being disrupted on my account. All my life, I had done everything I could not to stir up trouble. I had kept problems to myself. Unfortunately, circumstances were spiraling far beyond my control. My spirit was beaten down. I was exhausted. Something had to give. I was no longer happy with my life.

****

6:30 A.M., Saturday morning.

"Dr. Karos."

I opened my eyes. Dr. Hobbes was standing at my bedside.

"How are you feeling?"

I sat up and brushed my hair back with my fingers.

"I'm leaving the program," I said. I hesitated for a reaction but none came. "There're just so many things I want to do in my life. I mean- don't get me wrong- I love medicine, but even this is too limiting for me."

Dr. Hobbes dragged over a chair and sat down, his stethoscope hanging out his white coat pocket. He folded his hands and simply nodded.

"I think doing just one thing, anyone who does just one thing- even if he does it well- is placing boundaries around himself," I said. "Most people don't understand they're doin' it and eventually regret it. They regret they've put these...these limitations on their... their one and only life."

"You're saying no one should do one thing, professionally or otherwise, because it's imprisoning, and you're suggesting this is the case because?"

Dr. Hobbes wasn't going to let me get away with ambiguity, not even in my own hospital bed.

"Because there's nothing after this! This is it! Life's what's important, not what *might* happen after we die. Nothing might happen! It's about today. So why should anyone do just one thing? One profession? Devoting so much time to a single thing when there's so much out there doesn't make sense to me anymore. It's confining. Why should I just do medicine? There're so many other things I like, so many other things I wanna try."

Dr. Hobbes' tie was dark blue. In the light of dawn, it appeared ebony.

"Do you feel limited by your job or by something else?"

"What else?" I asked.

Dr. Hobbes didn't reply. He preferred I say it.

"Time? Do I feel limited by time because I got myself sick?" I said. "Yes, I do."

"Illness is part of life," he said. "Tell me, Dr. Karos, do you feel yourself more spiritual...?"

"But that's wrong! Isn't that wrong? You either believe or you don't believe. I have more respect for people who truly, truly believe in a God than those who only look for Him whenever they need Him. That's just selfish."

"Are you a good person, Dr. Karos?"

"I know I am."

"Why?"

"I guess because that's the way I was brought up."

"Here's a hypothetical. If you believed in God- for the sake of argument, if you did- would you fear Him?"

"No. Why should I? I've been good. I've lived a moral life."

"Then given that, there'd be no selfishness if you decided to one day ask for guidance. I for one am *not* impressed by those individuals who are good because they *fear* God. I *am* impressed by those people who are good because they love humanity."

"I'm one of those people."

"Then you were right all along. You have nothing to fear."

Dr. Hobbes was still talking, but I stopped listening. I had thirteen. *13. True goodness only comes from a love of humanity.* But was this consistent? Was this something *I* truly believed or was it merely something that sounded right because I had so much faith in Dr. Hobbes?

"But it doesn't make sense," I blurted out interrupting whatever it was he had been saying. "A lot of good people don't get a fair shake, and there's just no explanation, no reason for it. How can your God possibly be all-good given the way the world is? It doesn't fit! Why would Someone like that *allow* these things to happen to me? I've always tried to be a good person. I've always been a good person. So then why? Why should all this bad stuff happen to me? Tell me why!"

Dr. Hobbes reached deep into his soul and proceeded to break my heart: "I don't know why."

Chapter 26

When my parents walked in, I choked back tears. I hadn't seen them for over six months. Sleepless and exhausted from the flight, both appeared pale and more wrinkled than I remembered. Up until that moment, I hadn't realized how much I missed them, how much I needed them. My mother dropped her purse and sat down on the edge of my hospital bed, hugging me firmly with both arms, stroking my hair like she did when I was a child. I wanted to be a child again.

"Why didn't you call us?" she said with all of her Greek accent.

"We will get through this together," said my father.

"You're going to get better, every day stronger," my mother added. "I will not leave the hospital until we walk out together. I saw the waiting room. There is a couch. I will sleep there."

I smiled through the tears and let escape a sigh of relief.

"When you get better, we want you to come to Greece with us," my father said. "Enough with all this education. Fifty years of education! As far as I'm concerned, you're overeducated. And now it's work, work, work all the time. Enough! It's time to slow down."

"You are so busy and so distracted the last few years, we never see you anymore," said my mother.

I filled my parents in on the events of the past five weeks starting with the scalpel injury. They knew more than they let on. More relaxed than I had been in a week, the fatigue caught up with me and at some point I dozed off.

I was awakened by a deep, raspy voice. It must have been close to midnight. The attending hepatologist- an older gentleman with wavy white hair and a reliable Yale bowtie- was at the door to my room introducing himself to my parents. I had met him once while rotating on the transplant service and recalled having been impressed with his clinical judgment. He ushered my parents out into the hallway but kept them within earshot.

"Your son has early fulminant liver failure," the hepatologist said. "Up until a few years ago, we used to think that hepatitis C didn't cause it immediately upon contraction of the virus. Since then, a couple of reports have come out that support the fact that it can cause it. We have to keep a very, very close eye on him because things haven't stabilized yet. His bloodwork suggests that his condition may get worse before it gets better."

"Why is he so yellow?" asked my mother.

"That's one reason why we use the word 'fulminant.' It means a lot of his liver cells are failing. There is bile leaking out of the liver and ending up in the bloodstream and from there it gets deposited in the skin."

"But he's so young," my mother said.

"That should work in his favor- no question about it," said the hepatologist.

"He will get better," my father said.

"We hope so," said the hepatologist. "He waited a long time before coming into the hospital. He was malnourished and severely, severely dehydrated. Both of these factors worsened and weakened his immune system."

"He has μελανχολία," my mother said. "Do you know what this is?"

"Melancholy. Sure. It has Greek roots. I'm happy to say I retained something from my liberal arts education," the doctor laughed. "An imbalance of one of the four humors- what we now call depression. I know your son was taking anti-depressants and at a much higher dosage and frequency than he should have been and to some extent, I have no doubt, the pills also contributed to some of what we're seeing. This is well beyond what the virus usually does on its own." There was a brief silence. "The depression unfortunately hurt him quite a bit. It kept him from seeking medical attention sooner, and the remedy he was taking for it only made his liver function worse. We need to somehow address this depression as well while he's here, and I would probably suggest we have one of our psychiatrists come by and see him."

Another pause followed by my mother's voice: "We love our son very much, but the last few years he has been pushing us away. He has made it difficult for us to be a part of his life. Even when we visit, we only see him for a few hours, and he never comes to Greece to see us anymore. It's been years."

"He's a little bit of a loner," my father said. "He always has been. But he's a good boy."

"He has very few friends. I can't remember the last time he told us about one of his friends," my mother said.

"And he's very preoccupied with his own health," said my father. "He has a very strong fear of getting sick."

"As I said, we will definitely have one of our psychiatrists see him," said the hepatologist.

"Tell me doctor, how serious is this?"

"Mrs. Karos, I've been doing this for thirty years. It's rare to see rapid liver failure after such a recent acquisition of this virus. It's difficult for me to say how it will all play out."

Staring up at the shadows dancing around the ceiling, I wondered how many of my patients had heard my own whispers outside their rooms and regretted not being more careful and compassionate every single time. Under my breath, I counted from one to thirteen flinging each bead one at a time along the komboloi's strand. I kept the single leftover bead in my grasp wondering when I would finally be solving the puzzle.

Stuck in a hospital bed with the number thirteen hanging over my head! Lucky thirteen, I hoped. I rubbed the navy-colored 'mati' that hung next to the tassel between my thumb and index finger. One blue eye on the komboloi, two yellow eyes on a ghost, and somewhere a seer who had thrashed me with an evil eye. My life was filled with superstition, foolishness, irrationality. *How absurd.*

****

For a second straight night, I tossed and turned on the bumpy hospital mattress. Suddenly, I sprung up as if from a nightmare. I looked around the room and saw my mother resting in a chair next to my bed. I tapped her leg without a response, so I shook her vigorously until she opened her eyes.

"Mom, do me a favor. Check if I forgot a letter on my desk. I can't remember if I sent it. It was for my friend Miranda. I think I had a stamp, but I can't remember if I found one or if I sent it. If I didn't send it, can you mail it out? I'm not sure. I can't remember if I sent it."

My mother spent the next twenty minutes reassuring me she would look for the letter and mail it. In the process, she must have realized Miranda wasn't just another friend. I shut my eyes again and ran the beads slowly between my fingers taking slow deep breaths until I fell back asleep.

By dawn, the retching had returned, and I threw up the small amount of water they had allowed me to drink. The doctors inserted a tube through my nose into my stomach to help prevent any more vomiting. They became more concerned when I told them I was feeling short of breath and decided to transfer me to the intensive care unit. There, they hooked me up to more monitors and inserted a catheter into a large vein in my neck to better assess my hydration status. They placed a second catheter into my privates to trend my urinary output. Although I wasn't sleepy, I couldn't keep my eyes open. The skin on my forearms was golden. I didn't have the strength to move about my own bed. Through the procedures, reassurances, and down-time, *it* was constantly there, the devil by my side, another major episode tempered only by the fact that I was too exhausted and disoriented to fully appreciate the hopelessness.

The following day was a blur. I remember speaking to a psychiatrist briefly only to be told he would return when I was more awake and had more energy to speak with him. I could barely lift my arm up off the bed and slept most of the day. My parents and Philip were in and out in spite of the strict I.C.U. visiting hours.

At some point, Ted paid me a visit.

"Doin' OK?"

"Ted, I'm happy you're here. Can you call Dr. Hobbes?"

"Say that again. I don't understand."

"Can you call Dr. Hobbes? I need to talk to him."

"You need what?"

"Call him."

"I don't understand. Why don't you get some rest now?"

By late afternoon, my breathing became shallower. Although I had a face-mask on with a high amount of oxygen running through it, I could hear them talking about my oxygenation dropping on the monitor. I could feel the muscles in my neck tightening and bulging with every breath. My chest was rising and falling dramatically, and each respiration required great effort as if I were trying to suck air through a straw.

A sudden flurry of activity followed. Anesthesiology was called, and the team arrived immediately. Although I had my eyes shut, I could feel my bed being moved to the center of the room and sensed bodies all around me. Medications were being asked for. Boxes and packaging were being ripped open. More voices arrived- both male and female- and I felt the urgency in all of them.

"Dr. K, we're gonna put a breathing tube down."

"I can't breathe good," I gasped.

"I know, that's why we're gonna do this. I'm Dr. James from anesthesia. Go ahead and keep your eyes closed but listen to what I'm saying. Now that you're awake and can understand me, I need to explain some things to you, and I know you're a doctor and you understand a lot, but bear with me. Your breathing has gotten much worse, especially your ability to oxygenate your blood. You're working much harder than I'd like to see so we're gonna put the breathing tube in your airway.

"So how's it gonna feel with the tube down? Well, I can tell you as a physician but also as a former patient that it's not comfortable, so we're gonna do everything we can to keep you comfortable while it's in.

"We're gonna put you off to sleep now. I'm gonna give you a bit of a benzo just to relax you. You should already be feeling it. Once the tube is in, we'll continue to sedate you to keep you comfortable so you're gonna be a little groggy and disoriented most of the time."

No. NO! I only have thirteen!

"You'll probably dream a little bit so try and have good dreams. There may be times through all this when you may be more awake and times when you'll be fully asleep. If you're too awake, and we sense you're uncomfortable, we'll give you more sedatives to relax you. Truth is, once all this is over, I'll bet you won't remember much about this whole experience anyway. Once you're better, and we remove the tube, you'll probably remember things up until this point and everything in between will just be a blur or what you might call a stream of consciousness."

A stream of consciousness?

"OK, off to sleep you go."

Chapter 27

Tum...Fshhhhhhhhhhhhhhhhh
Uncle Timos lost his life at Brigham... I had my most productive
years there...
There? Here! The scene of the crime. Must be why they placed
me in wrist restraints.
Ridiculous.

****

They put me on the ventilator. But when? Was I intubated
yesterday? How much time has passed?
I'm choking with this tube down my throat. Can't talk. Can't stop
gagging. Can barely move. All I can do is think. I hate thinking so
much.
Tum...Fshhhhhhhhhhhhhhhhh
People I've loved. Lessons I've learned. This is what I'm seeing,
what's flashing through my mind, what's reflected in the stream.
Memories of those few I love... vivid...so vivid I'm reliving them.
But with the good comes the bad. Mixed in with my greatest
pleasures are my greatest pains, my most awful sorrows. And the rest?
Where is all the rest of my life? It's static.
Tum...Fshhhhhhhhhhhhhhhhh
"Dr. Karos, are you having any pain? ANY PAIN? Open your
eyes. OPEN YOUR EYES."
The Yale bowtie.
"Very good."
Mom.
Mom.
"We're here. We are not going anywhere."
I see my father.
And Philip.
My people who care.

"Ty, can you hear me?" Philip. "You convinced me, Ty. You're a great doctor. You always cared about your patients and now all these doctors are gonna take good care of you. Maybe I didn't always give doctors a fair shake, but these guys are doin' a great job, and you're gonna get better."

Dad.

Please don't cry.

Tum…Fshhhhhhhhhhhhhhhh

****

Atoms. I'm nothing more than atoms. My soul will disperse along with my body into the void. Atoms floating in random patterns inside a limitless universe. One universe out of countless. My essence won't vanish. I'll revert back to billions and billions of tiny little atoms. Maybe these bits will some day contribute to another man. Perhaps this is the true meaning of reincarnation.

Tum…Fshhhhhhhhhhhhhhhh

My genius Uncle Timos. With common sense, you made me believe in the religion of common sense. You taught me that I must reach out for happiness. I'm sorry. I'm so sorry.

Geoffrey Hobbes. I didn't lose perspective. I am good for I love humanity.

****

"Squeeze my hand. Dr. K, squeeze my hand! WIGGLE YOUR TOES. CAN YOU WIGGLE YOUR TOES?"

Tum…Fshhhhhhhhhhhhhhhh

Miranda and I. Two children playing in a pool of water underneath a halo moon making each other's life worth living.

Tum…Fshhhhhhhhhhhhhhhh

In the end, only the strongest emotions last. I wish I would have had more highs. Isn't that the whole point? To eliminate suffering. To shift the balance towards the good and the positive.

****

My komboloi. I can see my komboloi.

"He's waking up." My mother's voice. *"The doctors found a liver for you. Do you hear me? They have been searching for two weeks and now they have one. Do you understand me, Timo? Squeeze my hand if you hear me. They have a liver for you. This is great news."*

Tum...Fshhhhhhhhhhhhhhhh

****

How much time has passed? An hour? A day? A week? A month?
Tum...Fshhhhhhhhhhhhhhhh

"It's me- Phil. Ty, can you hear me? Can you hear me? Same as before- he doesn't hear us."

I know I have trouble believing, but I've lived a moral life, a decent life. I help the sick and less fortunate. I have compassion. I want to believe in You God, but it's so hard for me.

Tum...Fshhhhhhhhhhhhhhhh

I'm in the water now. Alone. My stars are dim. Have I enjoyed the journey?

****

"He asked for you." My mother's voice. *"He specifically asked for you. Timaki, Miranda is here to see you. She came all the way from Washington."*

Miranda?

"Miranda, you can talk to him. He can't talk because of the tube, but he's more awake today and he might understand you."

"We've lightened up his sedation, but in a few minutes we're gonna put him back down. He's still not ready to be weaned."

"Hi, Ty."

That sweet voice. Miranda. MIRANDA! I have always trusted my senses. My senses have guided me well. But I'm sad. I haven't had the chance to teach you what I've learned.

"I think he wants to write something down for you, Miranda. Your pad's right here."

Tum...Fshhhhhhhhhhhhhhhh

"And here's your pen. Open your fingers. Open your fingers. Now close them. Close them."

Miranda knows what I want to say to her, what I want to write to her.

Tum...Fshhhhhhhhhhhhhhhh

"Ty, I'm trying to read it. Is that an 'I'?"

I can't say it anymore.

"...love..."

I can't put it in a poem.

"...you."

All I can do is write it down.

"I love you too, Ty, and I want you to get better. You're gonna get better."

I've never kissed you. Now I can't even tell you how much I adore you. I feel you holding my hand. I knew you'd be there holding my hand.

Tum...Fshhhhhhhhhhhhhhhhh

Miranda, walk with me. Walk with me away from the superstitions of Delphi. Walk with me to the Garden. On the other side of the wall, I'll rescue you with common sense.

Tum...Fshhhhhhhhhhhhhhhh

"Ty, look what I brought."

Having you as my motivation helped me live fully. Having you as my inspiration made my life complete.

"Do you remember this pendant you gave me? I still have it. The pendant with the three circles. You remember it? I brought it."

Three intertwined circles. The Trinity has found its way back to me.

But why? Why now?

"I'm hanging it here on your bed...for good luck."

Luck? It has nothing to do with luck.

And what about the komboloi? There are secrets within my komboloi. There is meaning.

Tum...Fshhhhhhhhhhhhhhhh

Isn't there?

"Miranda, I think he wants you to have it."

"I shouldn't."

"He wants you to have it."

"Ty, are you sure? TY, ARE YOU SURE? You want me to have the worry-beads? Are you sure? OK. I'm taking it, and I'll treasure it. Thank you."

Your eyes are red. Don't cry.

Three words.

I need to write three more words for you.

Tum...Fshhhhhhhhhhhhhhhh

"Ty, I'm sorry I can't read that."

I need to write it.

Tum...Fshh

"Ty, I'm sorry. I can't read it."

I need to write it.

"I'm not sure what it says. Can anyone make it out?... Ty, I can't read it. I'm sorry... The letters are shaky. Why don't you rest now?"

I need to... Tum...Fshh... try again.

"Ty, I can't read it... You just drew a line."

Tum...Fshhhh...beep...beep...

Ringing?

"Why don't you rest now?"

A ringing noise.

"Sorry, everyone. He's getting a little agitated."

Bells.

"Why don't you all step outside for a few minutes until we can get him comfortable again."

Tum...Fshhhh...Tum

Don't go.

I'll write it again.

Just three words.

"Relax, Dr. K. You'll feel better in just a minute or two."

Don't ever forget to...

Tum...Fshh... Tum...Fshhhh...Tum

Live

For

Now

"Ty, get better. Oh, I got your poem in the mail. Thanks. Thank you."

My poem.

****

Envious of Youth

I was just in the playground
Yes, I was in the park
It was windy and the sand kept getting into my eyes
My red shovel was my favorite toy
I thought the other boy might want to dig a hole too
One next to mine and then we could connect them

But I don't know what happened

I was just in the playground
My mom was right over there, talking to that other lady
She's the mother of that old girl on the bicycle
The sun was in my eyes and it was pretty hot
My brother was on the silver swing
Maybe I should throw my tennis ball at him
Maybe he'll come and help me dig the biggest hole

I was there, in the playground, I'm sure of it
And I don't know how it happened
But somehow, I just didn't get a chance to finish.

****

Tum...Fshhhhh
'There's no reason to go at it alone.' That's what he told me at the station. And now I understand. He meant God.
Tum...Fshhhhh
The way out was directly in front of me. The radiance. The glow of the train. It was making its way over to me.
He meant God. I turned away. I was so afraid.
Watch over me. Please watch over me. That's all I ask of You. I'm afraid. I'm so afraid. The immortal soul is a delusion. I want to believe there's something else, but it's so difficult for me. So difficult. I love being young, but I hate being depressed and anxious all the time. Were You punishing me for my irreverence?
"Give him something and knock him out. And tighten his restraints! He's getting way too agitated and I'm getting tired of him pulling at everything. Dr. K! Calm down! CALM DOWN!"
Stop the pain. I can't take this pain any more.

Tum...Fshhhhhhhhhh

I try not to be afraid, but I'm terrified of not existing. I don't want to lose my ability to feel, to sense.

"The guy's dying. Come on man, give him a break. You heard what happened, right? Poor guy had a liver, but it fell through."

Too much pressure. Too much pain. It's making me sick.

"Why's that?"

Tum...Fshhhhhh

"The match was perfect, but apparently the donor family changed their minds and wouldn't give the transplant guys permission to harvest."

Fearing death is a cruel punishment.

Tum...Fsh...Tum...Tum...Fshhhhhh

"Why's that? Stop flailing! You're gonna hurt yourself!"

The death card was meant for me.

Tum...Fshh...Tum...Fshh

"They found out it went against the teachings of their church or something like that. Hey, catch him! He's gonna roll out of bed!"

Miranda. I think of you whenever I look up at the stars.

My little Miranda. My one true love. I met you when you were only fourteen.

Fourteen?

FOURTEEN.

FOURTEEN!!!!

Love is all that matters.

14. Love is all that matters.

LOVE IS ALL THAT MATTERS. The overwhelming memory that's reflected. Shining brilliantly. Like my stars, always radiant. The stream brought out my love for my little Miranda, my personal omphalos. Everything we do, we do for happiness, for pleasure, but especially for love.

But does it fit? Does it fit? It's not epicurean.

"I've been trying to prevent him from hurting himself since I came on shift. Sorry, but if he falls, he falls."

I'm falling?

Is this all there is for me?

Tum...Fshh...Tum

Will I erase?

Tum...beepbeepbeep

Can you die in your dreams?

Moonlight.

I'm naked.

The bed's soft. Immaculate white sheets to cover myself with.

The sound of waves splashing on the shore.

Beyond the open window: the sea transected by a full moon, a perfectly clear sky with the brightest stars I've ever seen.

"Hi, is Robert there?... His fiancée...Three weeks ago...Thank you, thank you so much."

A figure, lying next to me in the darkness, sleeping.

My eyes are adjusting: a thin woman, her back to me, laying there uncovered, in the nude. Dark hair. Smooth skin of her back. Her bare bottom.

Her breathing- so soft, so peaceful.

"Honey, I can't talk long because they don't allow cell phones...No, I'm just outside the room. The poor guy died."

Music, ever so light. A muffled sound. The beat's growing louder. Or is that me- my heart?

She's moving her shoulder. Now her legs. Turning her body towards me.

I know her perfect face. How I love that smile.

"It was weird and really awkward. His whole family was here. I felt completely out of place...But I told you- his mother called me...How would you have gotten out of it?"

My little brown-eyed girl. The greatest mystery of all.

"Are you OK, Ty?"

The sweet whisper of autumn leaves in a gentle breeze.

I fall in love all over again.

"He was a good guy- I mean, you know that- but I think he was a bit unstable... He said he loved me... No, he couldn't talk, he wrote it down... I know, I know... I'm telling you, honey... I'm telling you... No, I know it's ridiculous... Honey, I barely knew him. I barely knew him."

Acknowledgments

I must recognize the following groups and individuals:

My supporters

Thank you to my wife Rosalia and my two girls, who provided me with the support and motivation to pursue this hobby of mine in the plethora of free time I've had over the last decade.

Thank you to my parents and my brothers Costas and Mark for providing me with the early environment and experiences- through childhood, adolescence, and young adulthood- which shaped me into the person who I am today.

Helen Ellis

Thank you to Helen. I am indebted to my fellow writer and friend for helping pave the way as a story began to take shape. Her sound advice early in the process was critical. Helen showed me how novel-writing is done and gave me the positive feedback I needed to continue. There wouldn't have been a finished novel without her wisdom.

My mentors

The Cathedral School, the Browning School, NYU, Downstate, and Yale deserve much thanks for challenging and developing the four-year old brain I had before they all started teaching me stuff.

Thank you to Mr. Ingrisani for improving my English reading/writing skills many full moons ago. Language *is* power which explains why most of us were intimidated by you back then (in a positive way of course).

Thank you to Gotham Writers' Workshop (especially Diana, Marcy, and my classmates) who helped me 'fine-tune' during our weekly evening sessions.

My wonderful critics

Thank you to Stephan, Mike, Sylvia, Lex, Judy, and Pauline for reviewing early drafts of the manuscript and providing thoughtful suggestions.

Starbuck's

Thanks for providing Helen and me a venue to sit and discuss. Places *to stop and think and talk and drink* are vital. Without leisure time to contemplate and *reflect*, we live to work rather than work to live.

About the Author

Spiros G. Frangos is a Yale-trained surgeon specializing in trauma, emergency general surgery, and surgical critical care. He lives in Manhattan with his wife and two daughters. This is his first novel.

www.ingramcontent.com/pod-product-compliance
Lightning Source LLC
Chambersburg PA
CBHW030519020726
47494CB00004B/1157